GEMMA FOWLER

CITY OF
RUST

Chicken House

2 PALMER STREET, FROME, SOMERSET BA11 1DS

Gemma Fowler has asserted her right under the Copyright, Designs and Patents Act 1988 to be identified as the author of this work.

Cover and interior design by Steve Wells
Cover and interior illustration by Karl James Mountford
Spheres illustration by Gemma Fowler
Typeset by Dorchester Typesetting Group Ltd
Printed and bound in Great Britain by CPI Group (UK) Ltd, Croydon, CR0 4YY

The paper used in this Chicken House book is made from wood grown in sustainable forests.

1 3 5 7 9 10 8 6 4 2

British Library Cataloguing in Publication data available.

PB ISBN 978-1-910655-43-6
eISBN 978-1-913322-90-8

To Frank,
for all the adventures ahead.

Also by Gemma Fowler

Moondust

THE SPHERES

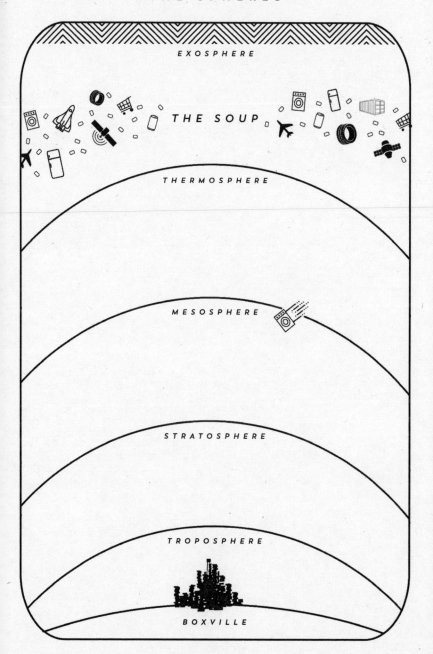

EXOSPHERE

THE SOUP

THERMOSPHERE

MESOSPHERE

STRATOSPHERE

TROPOSPHERE

BOXVILLE

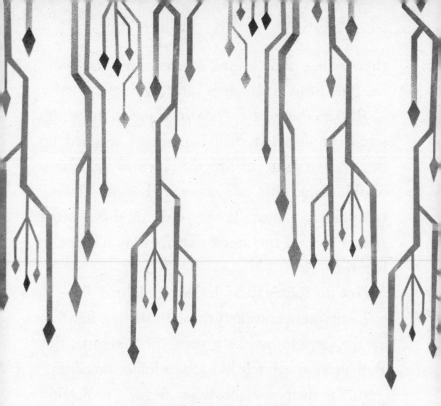

BOXVILLE

In the shadows by the vending machines, Railey peered out of the gap between her jacket collar and her fringe.

Night had finally cast its shadow over the great container city of Boxville, bringing it back to life after the heat of the day.

Around her, dusty traders hung out of the kiosks that ringed the arena, shouting and showing their wares, trading junk of every type you could imagine from under their tatty awnings.

Above them the containerblocks, towering stacks of jumbled steel containers, reached up into the dark sky, turning the city into a claustrophobic labyrinth of hot metal and glowing tungsten and dust. It was only in these wider streets around the arena that there was space to breathe.

Not for Railey though. Not tonight.

Excitement travelled through the air, lighting up the passers-by like a string of firelights. But Railey's stomach felt like it was full of sandflies.

In the dusty air above her head, a projection was quietly counting down the minutes until the race, washing the arena in its cool green light. Thirty minutes. Where was Atti? If he didn't show up soon, they were going to be late.

A familiar queasy feeling rose in her stomach; she swallowed it back quickly. She didn't have time for nerves tonight. 'Come on,' she whispered to the vending machine.

The ancient mechanisms inside clunked as it finally processed her order. Railey listened, imagining the old oiled cogs and narrow chutes inside turning a perfect, pre-programmed dance, putting the ingredients together in the same way they had done all day, every day since it had been made. Railey loved the old vendors – they were survivors, like Gran.

Boxville was a city made from the scraps. Everything here had lived a hundred lives before, they had been made, then unmade and then remade again – the buildings, the clothes, the food, even the people. Only the vendors remained unchanged, chugging out the same fizzing drinks that rotted your teeth day in, day out for more years than Railey could imagine.

The vendor clunked one last time and a clear, egg-shaped biocarton bounced into the chute, followed by a surge of fizzing yellow liquid. Railey grabbed the carton and sat down at one of the rotted plastic tables, eyes fixed on the count-down. Twenty-eight minutes. Her stomach flies multiplied.

A bright yellow gecko appeared on the end of the table. It gazed up at her with deep-blue eyes flecked with gold, like sparkling galaxies. The word 'PROTOTYPE' was stamped across its fat tail.

The gecko pulled the straw of Railey's drink down and took a long draw of the fizzy pop.

'What time do you call this, Atti?' Railey said, pulling the straw out of its mouth. 'And you know you shouldn't do that. If somebody sees you . . . Plus, it's *mine*.'

'I ran into a tiny problem,' the gecko said, holding in a burp.

Railey felt a stab in her guts.

'What kind of problem?'

A cry of anguish echoed down the street.

Atti let the burp out. 'That kind.'

Railey ran as fast as her mouldy trainers would carry her, through the forest of dusty legs towards the source of the cry.

'Quick!' the gecko whispered from inside her collar.

Railey slipped on the dirt as a fat grazing SteelSheep stepped into her path. It eyed her with disinterest for a second, flashing its alloy teeth, then went back to grazing on a rusted hubcap. Railey leap-frogged over its wire wool hide, and landed with a splash in a puddle of watery grease running from a nearby synth burger kiosk.

A crowd had gathered around the source of the commotion – a hundred or so dusty Boxville street traders, their backpacks and jackets heaving with illegal objects, traded and soon-to-be-traded and instantly forgotten about at the sound of the scream.

Railey could even see the silhouettes of the containerblock residents, peering curiously over their balconies high above.

'This way,' the gecko whispered again, directing her around the back to where the crowd was thinner. 'She's really done it this time.'

Railey pushed through the crowd to get a look. When she did, she felt the blood drain from her face.

An elderly woman was stood in the centre of the crowd shouting at the top of her voice. A huge wrench gleamed in her white-knuckled fist, swaying just above the greasy head of a trader Railey knew from one of the plastics stalls. He was cowering in the dust at the woman's slippered feet.

'Oh no. Gran, not now.' A burning sensation ran through Railey – a familiar mixture of humiliation and deep, deep love.

Gran's violet boiler suit was grey with dirt and her hair was a matted mess on top of her head, framed by her precious SmartGoggles.

'The skies'll burn thanks ter the likes of you!' Gran was shouting. 'Skies and cities and all and everything! I know you Junkers better'n the others, remember that. I got half your blood!'

The boy held up his arms to protect his face.

'I int no Junker!' he shouted, looking to the crowd for help. He wouldn't find any – Boxville traders minded their own business.

'This is what happens when you don't feel the dirt between yer toes,' Gran continued, 'up there in the Spheres yer can't feel the weight of yer actions . . .'

'I never been off the ground, Gran! It's Krys! Little Krys from the market, I'm the one what trades yer yer tubs and toothbrushes—'

'Enough!' Gran shouted. Her arms shook as

she raised the wrench above her head.

There was a hard nip on Railey's neck. 'What are you waiting for, Railey?' Atti said. 'Stop her before she kills him!'

Railey took a deep breath and stepped out of the crowd.

'Gran?'

Railey ignored the quiet jeers from the traders. She smiled reassuringly as Gran's eyes flicked to hers. 'Time to go home, Gran.'

Gran kept the wrench high above Krys's head.

'Get this mad hoover bag away from me!' Krys shouted to Railey.

'Let's see Gran nobble Krys first though,' a trader shouted.

'Yeah, go on Gran, gi him a good hiding!'

Laughter rippled through the crowd. Gran looked around her, blinking her black pebble eyes. It was a look Railey knew well – the real world was coming back to her.

'That my Railey, is it?' she said softly, then grinned wickedly. 'Got me some good trade in there, girl?' She tapped Railey's pockets with the wrench.

'Course I have, Gran,' Railey said, grabbing her arm gently. 'I'll show you if you like, but not with all these traders watching.'

Gran winked. 'Good girl.'

Railey smiled. 'C'mon then.' She looked down at her feet, where Krys was still cowering.

'You can get lost now,' she said, kicking dust at him.

'Oh! Hello there, Krys love,' Gran said, as if he'd just appeared out of nowhere. 'What you covered in dust for? Yer dad'll lose his nut ter see you like that on race day.'

Krys opened his mouth to complain, but Railey prodded him. 'Go.'

Krys dusted down his old sweatshirt. 'Not without me wrench. Crazier than a dog in the sun, that one. An' better off keepin' her on a leash too.'

Railey gently tugged the wrench from her Gran's hand and threw it at Krys's feet, aiming to clip one of his toes.

'Ow!'

'Get lost.'

The crowd had begun to disperse, only a few

of the older traders remaining – the ones who leant on sticks, who remembered and respected Gran from the days when she ruled the Junk Market with trade from the most dangerous junking clans.

Gran was as good as legend in the market, and famous right from the dusty streets of Boxville to the crystalline towers of Glass City. All because she was half Junker, and her mixed blood meant the clans would give her the best trade – junk picked right out the Soup, the endless band of rubbish that orbited the Earth.

But those days were just memories now. Gran's steel-toe-capped slippers hadn't stepped into the Junk Market in the city's rooftops since the last monsoon.

Railey directed Gran back into the throes of the crowds, keeping her head on her shoulder.

The green glow of the countdown coated the crowds as they walked back towards the arena, turning bodies into black silhouettes and the junk stalls into shadows. Railey's heart clenched.

'Oh no, Atti,' she whispered, 'only fifteen minutes left!'

She clutched her backpack and pulled Gran's arm gently.

'Feels like it's too late,' Gran said with a sob.

Railey and Atti exchanged a glance. Gran was in no fit state to make her own way home . . . so she would just have to come with them.

'We've got time, Gran,' Railey reassured her as they hurried into the arena. 'Just got to go a bit faster.'

Atti popped his head out of Railey's collar and jumped on to Gran's shoulder.

'Two races left, Gran,' he whispered right in her ear. 'It's all to play for!'

Gran giggled. 'Oh Atti! My little pilot. Best thing these old hands ever made.'

Atti grinned. Railey rolled her eyes and tapped her backpack. 'The Fox is the best thing you ever made, Gran,' she said, looking at the gecko, 'mainly because it don't answer back.'

A pounding electronic beat began to thump its way across the ground.

'BOXVILLE,' the Starter's voice echoed all around them, 'THE BETTING KIOSKS ARE NOW CLOSED. THE PENULTIMATE

DRONE RACE OF THE WORLD-FAMOUS BOXVILLE SERIES WILL BEGIN IN TEN MINUTES.'

They were just in time.

THE PITS

Railey made her way to the tatty chicken wire fence that separated the raceway from the stands. She plonked Gran down on an upturned bucket and put her hands on her soft, wrinkled cheeks.

'Gran?' she said, taking the SmartGoggles out of the old woman's cloudy hair.

'Yes, my love?'

'We're going now. You can watch the race from here, right at the front. Just – don't move. OK?'

The crowds were spilling in all around them, taking their seats and chattering excitedly about bets and drone stats and trades. Gran glanced around and clutched at her cardigan nervously.

'Don't worry,' Railey said, pointing to a cluster of black boxes that hung over the racetrack just to their left. 'That's the flyers' box right there. That's where we'll be racing. You'll be able to keep your eye on us the whole time.'

'Oh, that's good, my love,' Gran nodded. Her eyes were pointed at Railey's face, but they weren't really *looking*.

Railey sighed and kissed her forehead and reluctantly turned away. As she did, she noticed a girl watching her from the shadows. She was as skinny as a rake, with a tangled mop of blonde curls covering most of her face.

'I like your pet,' she said, pointing to Atti, who was perched on her shoulder. Railey felt light-ning in her veins and pushed Atti back into her collar.

'Just a desert lizard,' she said quickly.

'Yeah, right.' The girl rolled her big, watery eyes and disappeared into the crowd.

Railey watched for a second, thinking the girl seemed strange, then shook herself. She didn't have time for this.

Pulling Gran's SmartGoggles over her eyes, she ran as fast as she could around the fence to the flyers' box, and shouldered open a large buckled door with 'PITS' written over it in dribbling paint.

She stepped from the dusty heat of the arena into the dark quiet of a huge underground hangar packed with teams huddled around glowing white workbenches. Quiet as she could, she made her way to the only bench that was left clean of parts, placed her pack on to the glowing surface and sank to the floor.

They'd made it.

Atti's feet padded down her arm. Railey checked that no one was watching, and then wrapped her arms around her legs, letting her hair cover the gecko in a black curtain.

'You're breathing like a bull, Railey.'

'She's getting worse, Atti. She could've killed Krys—'

The gecko huffed. 'It wouldn't be a great loss.'

'Atti—'

'I know.'

Railey's heart was fluttering, and it was making her shake. The last thing she needed now was shaking hands.

Atti shifted forward and pushed his snout against the tip of her nose. Together, they took two deep breaths.

'Let's make it tomorrow's problem, OK?' the gecko said, placing a cold, squidgy hand on her cheek. 'Tonight is for racing and winning, and wiping that smile right off—'

'There's the loser,' interrupted another voice.

Railey's head shot up, sending Atti scurrying under the table and into the pack where their drone was stashed. A boy was standing over her. From this angle he seemed as wide and solid as a containerblock.

Welt.

'Almost din't make it this time,' he said in a voice that sounded like he needed to clear his throat.

Railey sprang to her feet, the presence of her rival like smelling salts. Welt stepped up close enough that she could feel his breath on her forehead.

'But I did,' she said, shoving him away – he stumbled, even though she was half his size. 'That's what matters.'

He glowered. No loving mother or father would call their son after a skin condition, but no one could deny Welt looked like his name. He was big and reddish and swollen, sweating constantly into clothes that were always too warm for the weather. Railey knew why Welt dressed for a winter that never came to Boxville.

Drone parts.

Drone racers carried their spare parts on them at all times, in secret pockets stitched into heavy, oversized jackets.

Railey licked her lips. She'd love to take a look at what Welt had stashed in his white iguana-hide jacket. Her own racing jacket was crammed with whatever she'd been able to scavenge, but drone racers needed lots of parts and parts were expensive trade, more than Railey could manage from the meagre supplies left gathering dust in Gran's workshop.

Welt smiled, revealing a set of teeth remade from plastic Scrabble board tiles.

'It dun't matter.' He crossed his thick arms and shut his massive cow eyes. 'This year's series is a done deal.'

'That right, is it?' Railey pulled the rusty casing of their racing drone from the backpack and laid it on the bench.

The Fox. Railey looked at her racing drone lovingly. She knew every degree of every angle on its boxy body, she'd calculated and honed and balanced the internal motors for hours with Gran – who became as sharp as a razor whenever the drone needed attention.

The Fox looked nothing like the other drones in the series – it was bigger, bulkier, made to Gran's old exacting blueprints. It didn't even look like it should fly at all, let alone win the series, but it was good enough – and Welt knew it.

Railey pushed the collapsed rotor blades into position with a satisfying *pop*.

'Even if you can get the Destroyer to fly better than a drunken sky squirrel and actually win this race, the points'll still make the series a tie – remember?'

She turned around, holding the Fox to her chest like a baby. Welt stood in her way, his fists clenched. She could practically hear the big guy's brain ticking like an old clock. 'Move. Please.'

His face settled into a sneer.

'If it's a tie, then it'll go right down ter the final race.'

Railey glanced around the pits. The other competitors were trying to look busy, but she felt their ears swivelled on to their conversation like SAT dishes.

'Yeah. If it comes to it,' she conceded.

Welt leant down so his face was level with Railey's.

'It will.' He looked down at the Fox and Railey clutched it closer. 'An' when it does, we'll 'ave yer little secret spilling out all over the pit floor – whatever it is.'

He flicked the Fox's blades with a fat finger and Railey felt a delicate weight inside shift. She snarled up at Welt, 'It's sad. You want the Fox more than you want the series.'

Welt stepped even closer. 'It dun't make sense. It dun't even look like a proper racer. We think you got something stitched inside it, something illegal that yer nutty gran traded from them inbred Junkers.'

He prodded the Fox again. He was lucky Railey had her hands full, otherwise she'd shove her multitool in his eye.

'There's no secret,' she lied. 'I'm just a better tech than you. Get over it, the others have.'

'No they ain't. They just dun't have the guts ter say it.'

A shiver ran over her.

'You got no friends in the pits,' Welt snorted. 'You ain't got friends anywhere—'

'RACERS!' the speakers dotted around the hangar coughed. 'Please make your way to the flyers' box.'

Railey dodged past Welt's legs before he could continue, and made her way through the teams of suspicious techs and engineers to the ramp that led to the flyers' box. She didn't bother looking back – she knew Welt wouldn't be far behind. She would be sharing the flyers' box with him soon enough, but she needed distance, just for a few minutes.

A familiar tight feeling grew in her chest. She tried to shake it off, but the more she focused on it the more it grew – Welt was right, there was something hidden inside their drone. Something that would have them disqualified in an instant if anyone found out. Truth was, the Fox wasn't flown remotely from a tablet like the others – it had controls, and a tiny gecko pilot. Atti. Gran called him their secret weapon.

She moved the Fox to one arm and wiped her sweating palms on her jeans. Why did she let Welt get to her? Right before the race, too?

She took a deep breath. It was OK. No one would ever find out about Atti, because she made sure no one ever got close to the Fox. She'd stick them with her multitool if anyone ever tried.

The weight of the drone shifted again, and Railey had to hoist it up on to her shoulder.

'What's going on?' Atti's voice was muffled through the thin metal.

'Nothing. Just Welt being Welt.'

'When's his dad going to send him out to the solar farms where he belongs?'

Railey grinned. 'Next year. Why do you think he needs this title so much?'

The voice chuckled quietly.

Railey made her way up a steep ramp that opened out into a long room with huge windows that overlooked the raceway. Thirty flyers' booths ran along the window, each fitted with a narrow chute that led out into the arena below.

Railey placed the Fox at the top of her chute and pulled Gran's SmartGoggles over her eyes.

Beyond the mirrored glass windows stood a complicated tangle of neon and steel: the raceway. It rose up out of the compacted dust on hundreds of twisted steel struts, remade from the carcasses of aeroplanes, broken up by flickering neon hoops, narrow steel tunnels and slow-moving pincers. From the height of the flyers' box, it looked like the dusty spine of a long-dead alien whale.

The crowd behind the fence was bigger than

any she'd seen before. People were piled on every surface available: lounging on containerblock roofs, hanging off balconies and perched precariously on the awnings of shops and betting kiosks.

Railey felt a strange calm descend. She felt the protection of the raceway. Here, she wasn't Railey the Stray, or Railey the Trader, or the girl you went to when Gran was having one of her turns. Here, things were black and white. Working or not working. Winning or losing.

The races meant everything to Gran – they didn't have much else. It was what they lived for, every minute of every day.

Railey examined the circuit, using the goggles to zoom in on the neon hoops and scan the twisting tunnel of the figure of eight. The layout of the raceway changed for every race – that way, no racer gained an advantage over another. The SmartGoggles displayed the degree of the angles and the widths of the new track – this circuit had obviously been designed to test them.

Railey crouched down, pretending to examine the drone's rotor blades.

'Standard follow-the-rainbow circuit,' Atti's

reptilian voice whispered from inside.

Railey nodded and followed the hoops from red through the colour spectrum to violet, imagining the Fox whizzing perfectly through the dead centre of each. No time penalties, no obstructions.

'We'll have to tilt in the tunnels,' Atti said. 'They've made them smaller. The fans will kick back in the ridges—'

Welt burst into the room with a gust of air, his own goggles glowing in red circles in the half-light. Railey felt all her calm evaporate at the sight of him.

Atti huffed. 'I told you you'd made the fans too wide. You're obsessed with power . . . we'll lose seconds in there.'

Railey stuck her finger in the back of the drone, pretending to fiddle with the wires.

'Ouch.'

'Stop distracting me.'

'You nearly took my eye out—'

She glanced at Welt, and caught his eyes flicking from her back to the raceway.

'—because, of course, why do I need eyes.'

'Stop talking.'

'Why don't *you* stop talking?'

'Because humans can speak.'

'Well, that's a matter of opinion.'

'Atti . . .'

There was another clang of footsteps. 'Who are you talking to?'

Railey looked up. The Starter had entered the flyers' box.

Railey's back snapped straight like a container steel. 'No one, ma'am.'

Awkwardly tall and lavishly dressed, the Starter reminded Railey of the flamingos that sometimes appeared in the desert outside the city. 'Better to keep your strategy to yourself, y'know,' she said, rubbing her thin hands together as she positioned herself in her seat at the centre of the arc of racers. 'Big race, this one. The penultimate race of the series.'

Welt was squished so close to Railey she could smell the stink of his pits and the tang of his breath.

'Dun't matter,' he sneered. 'No strategy is gonna beat the Destroyer tonight.'

'I'd concentrate on the race, Welt,' Hemel, the boy on the other side of Welt, muttered. 'Isn't your dad sending you to the solar farms if you don't win this year?'

'Especially if you lose to a heap of junk like the Fox.' Katia, a racer who wore goggles with anime video screens, put her head up from a few booths down.

The big guy's fists clenched.

The Starter held out her hand.

'Enough now.' She pulled a tablet from her jacket and dusted it down with bejewelled fingers. 'Save your grievances for the circuit. The rules say no talking before the race – and no one is above the law here.' She tapped the mic button on her screen and the box lit up with grey light. 'In fact,' she murmured, 'we're all very much under it.'

Railey smiled. Boxville's drone races were illegal, technically, but Glass City had always turned a blind eye – Gran always said it was because they all had bets on the drones, and that they thought it kept people's minds on things other than trading with Junkers and causing trouble. People like her.

But then, Gran said a lot of things.

Railey flicked open the app that controlled the Fox. Her fingers were a third of the size of Welt's, but they were designed for soldering, not swiping delicately and precisely against a screen. Welt knew it too, and she could feel his eyes on her as she clumsily directed the Fox into the chute a metre in front of her.

Outside of the flyers' box, the crowd bayed. Every one of them had bets on the race, especially after the drama of the series so far.

Railey smiled. No one thought a heap of parts like the Fox would be able to compete with the slick Destroyer. But Railey and Gran had worked hard during the early races, shaving a hair's breadth off the blades, tightening the belt in the motor by one turn of the screw. Each time it flew the Fox had got faster, nippier, more reliable—

'What you grinning at?' Welt snorted.

Railey just shook her head and shifted her gaze back to the raceway.

The dusty beams of the projectors criss-crossed the course, casting live feeds on to the surrounding containerblock walls. They flicked from the profiles of the racers, to close-up drone's-eye views of the circuit. The crowd's cheers had turned into impatient chants. It was nearly time.

Railey's whole body hummed; she stood on her tiptoes, swaying left and right, letting the chanting, cheers and whoops of the crowd batter against her body like the wind. She lived for this.

Behind Railey, the Starter took a breath.

'The gates are open.' Her voice bounced around the arena. 'Now RACE!'

The lights turned green.

The chutes opened.

The roar of the crowd hit Railey like a tidal wave.

She let out a long, euphoric laugh and, as deftly as her fingers would allow, she flicked the Fox's controls over to the secret gecko pilot sitting inside it.

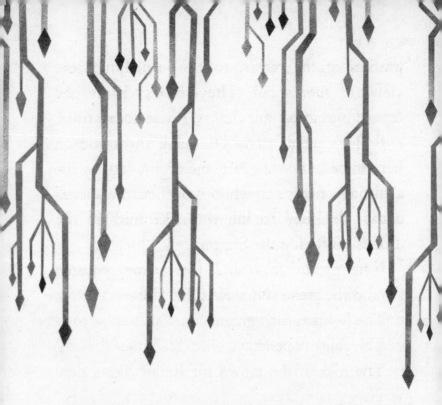

THE SECRET WEAPON

As soon as the drones dropped out of the chutes on to the raceway, Railey felt the surge of energy inside the arena. The crowd pushed hard against the fence, chanting and cheering as the lightning-fast drones sped through the twists and turns of the track.

Soon, the high whine of a klaxon marked the twentieth lap, and the part of the race everyone was waiting for – the use of the drones' traps.

The traps were booby traps, hidden within the drones, designed to sabotage their competitors during the race – flashes of light that caused temporary blindness, fiery rocket boosts that set alight any drones flying in their wake, blackout bombs designed to kill the electronics in the drones' motors.

Instantly the air around the raceway became filled with smoke and flashes and vibrations from the booby traps. Every time a trap was used it would send the crowd into a fence-shaking frenzy.

They weren't disappointed tonight.

By lap thirty-four, twenty drones were lying in pieces in the dust and the Fox and the Destroyer were flying blade to blade.

Railey held her breath. The rusty orange of the Fox blurred with the deep teal of the Destroyer as they skimmed the steel skeleton of the circuit, weaving in and out of each other's slipstreams, trying to force the other over the edge to incur a penalty. Her thumbs worked at the controls, flicking switches and pressing buttons, matching as closely as possible the tiny ship's movements. But it was all a game – Atti was the one in control.

The gecko was having an excellent race. The Fox swept gracefully through the rainbow-coloured hoops and dived up and down and out of the covered tube of the figure of eight with such precision that she would have clapped if she hadn't had to pretend to use the controls.

But Welt was cleverer than he looked. Each time the Destroyer gained air between it and the Fox, it released bursts of electricity towards Atti, forcing the Fox to dodge and weave to avoid a hit.

But the Fox had a few tricks of its own – one of the best and most technical traps in the series. The crowd were waiting for it, Railey could tell, because they cheered louder than she had ever heard them when Atti finally released the tiny harpoon hidden inside the Fox's nosecone.

It shot from its hatch and caught the tail of the Destroyer, piercing its carbon fibre body and dragging it violently backwards. Atti used the momentum of the harpoon to propel the Fox forwards, sending the Destroyer spinning off the track.

The speaker system screeched. '. . . And the Fox steals the lead with a sneaky little trick! Look at the slipstream readings there, enough to cause serious damage to the Destroyer's blades, but Welt is skilled enough to hold her steady, wait, and . . . into the loop in a perfect line . . . but is it enough to catch up with the Fox? Not if the last race is anything to go by!'

Inside the flyers' box, Railey could feel Welt's gaze flicking from her to the raceway. He definitely suspected something.

'I'd fix my eyes on the course if I were losing,' said Railey.

The screens around the raceway flicked back to the Destroyer and the crowd roared as it exited the loop.

'. . . Gaining ground,' the Starter's voice echoed, '. . . surely too fast . . . turning, lovely line through the hoops . . . And . . . oh! An unbelievable move from the Destroyer!'

Railey gasped. The Destroyer had cut across the Fox's path into the first of the rainbow hoops, sending the orange drone flying out of the circuit perimeter. The section of lights blinked red.

'. . . Forced penalty for the Fox— Wait! What's this? The Fox is already back on the Destroyer's tail, and they're headed into the figure of eight *together*!'

Railey pulled forward. 'No,' she muttered. 'There's not enough room.'

The two drones disappeared into the covered figure of eight section.

Railey held her breath.

Then, the arena plunged into darkness.

Railey looked down at her tablet. The screen was black as the sky. She pressed buttons and flicked the screen – but it was dead. Everything was dead – the lights, the projectors, the neons, the drones . . .

She tried to blink the darkness away, but all she could see through the windows was the outline of the raceway and the edges of the containerblocks reflecting the moonlight.

Silence crept over the arena like a fog, only to be broken by the deafening screech of metal on metal.

Sparks flew out of the figure of eight, lighting the surrounding track for a second, then dousing back to black. It was just long enough for Railey to catch the flash of orange and teal as the two drones skidded out of the tube and launched, out of control, towards the fence at the far side of the arena.

'No!' she and Welt both cried at the same time.

Without thinking, Railey jumped into the drone chute.

'No you dun't!' Welt shouted, grabbing at her jacket. 'Yer'll get the race voided if you get on the raceway!'

Railey slid down the chute, pulling Welt along with her. She didn't care about him or the race; she just had to know that Atti was OK.

They toppled out together into the dust beneath the raceway. Welt tried to grab her again, but she dodged his grip and ran as fast as she could between the hundreds of metal struts, kicking aside the shrapnel of the other drones, stumbling and crawling to the place where the Fox had come to a shattering stop.

'Oi!' Welt cried, giving chase.

'Atti!' she shouted. 'ATTI!'

From the outside, Atti was a gecko – same as all the other geckos that warmed their bellies on the city's hot corrugated metal walls – but Gran had made his insides out of computer parts. Their drone was broken into bits, and the thought that Atti could be in bits too was almost too much for Railey's heart to bear—

'Railey?' A small voice said from somewhere by her feet. 'Did we win?'

Railey looked down and relief flooded her body.

Atti stumbled on two legs, holding his head in his hands. He took two wobbly steps back and blinked his galaxy eyes in the dark.

'Oh Atti!' Railey went to pick him up, but stopped. The gecko was looking at something behind her.

'Yer a cheat!' Welt shouted, skidding to a stop. 'I knew there were something! Stinking CHEATS!'

'Ignore him,' Railey said, inspecting the gecko for injuries. 'Are you OK?'

'I don't think we should,' Atti said, woozily.

'He's got a gun.'

'What?'

Railey spun around.

A shape was emerging out of the dusty shadows behind Welt. A man, dark as the night but for two round green lenses that glowed where his eyes should be.

Railey froze.

'Doesn't look very friendly,' Atti slurred, before collapsing into the dust.

The man stepped out of the shadow.

He looked more robot than man – half his face was masked by remade night-vision goggles, and one of his arms had been replaced by something bigger and stronger and robotic, made of twisting carbon fibre tendons that flexed as he walked.

Welt gave a strangled yelp and ran away into the dark of the raceway.

The man raised his robotic arm. There was something short and wide and metallic clutched in its metal hand.

A PunchGun.

A weapon that compressed air into a fist and threw it at you with the force of a tornado. Railey had heard about them before, but she'd never seen one with her own eyes until now.

She scooped Atti up from the dust. When she stood up she realized the gun was pointed at something over her shoulder.

'Get away from them, yer good-fer-nothing scorpion.'

Railey spun on her heels.

Gran was standing behind them, the knife attachment on her multitool raised, and a gaping hole in the chicken wire fence behind her.

'Give me the pilot,' the man said, in a voice deep enough to have its own echo.

'I remember when Junkers used ter fight their own battles,' Gran shouted, 'not send the likes o' you to do it for 'em!'

Her stick was gone, and she looked tall and strong and powerful in her overalls, despite the fluffy cardigan that she wore over the top.

'The pilot comes with me,' the man said, holding out his human hand towards Railey. With the other he charged up the PunchGun with an electronic *thwarp*.

'Get down, Railey!' Gran shouted.

Railey fell to the floor. She felt the air above her ripple and bulge with the force of the Punch-Gun and a cry came from the crowd as the air pulsed above their heads.

'OK. I asked nicely . . .' the man said, then lunged forward.

'Railey!' Gran cried.

Railey stumbled back into Gran's hot, heavy arms.

'. . . Technical error . . .' The Starter's voice erupted out of the speakers like thunder.

A giant version of them was being broadcast shakily on the giant screens.

'What's this? The course has been invaded!' The Starter's voice stumbled. 'Oh, and . . . another . . . Spheres above, is that a Runner?'

'A Runner?' Railey exclaimed in disbelief, as Gran moved in front of her.

The Runners were bounty hunters, lawless and stateless, and famous for being bloodthirsty and ruthless and as dark and silent as the shadows.

The crowd had surged against the fence, spilling out of the hole and on to the track around Railey and Gran.

The Runner let out a cry, and ran towards them.

'Stay put, my love,' Gran whispered, then launched her old body towards the Runner as fast as her steel-toe-capped slippers would carry her.

'What's she doing?' Atti squeaked in Railey's ear. 'He'll blast her right out of the city!'

'. . . Please, can we calm down . . .' The Starter's voice crackled out of the speakers. 'There is no need for violence . . . please.'

Gran dropped into the dust and skidded the last few metres, slamming into the Runner's ankles like a bowling ball. As he fell to the floor, Gran twisted up sharply, gripping his robotic arm with one hand and jamming her multitool deep into its metal armpit with the other.

He cried out as his arm twitched, then swung violently upwards, sending him flying up into the air after it in a shower of golden sparks.

Gran rolled away and ran back towards Railey.

'Better get gone now,' she shouted breathlessly.

'What did you do?' Atti exclaimed.

'Switched it to automatic,' Gran panted.

Behind her, the bounty hunter staggered around, trying to regain control of his arm as it punched and whipped and twisted in the air around him.

'Quick now,' she said, pulling Railey back towards the fence. 'That's a military arm, that. Murderous things them, when they're left to their own devices . . . best get out its way.'

The crowd around them were running this way and that, screaming as the furious AI that Gran had unleashed inside the Runner's arm slapped and pulled and smashed at anyone and anything that got in its way.

Gran and Railey zigzagged through the crowd like sand snakes until they had enough space to run.

'That was amazing!' Atti cried, clinging onto Railey's shoulder. 'How did you know it would do that?'

'I din't,' Gran wheezed. 'And I'm figuring it won't last long neither, so we'd better be off before he gets control of it again.'

'But . . .' Railey looked back at the bright chaos of the raceway. 'The Fox, the series . . .?'

'It dun't matter no more,' Gran replied, turning away from the arena down a dark, narrow alley. 'They sent a Runner after us. None of it matters any more.'

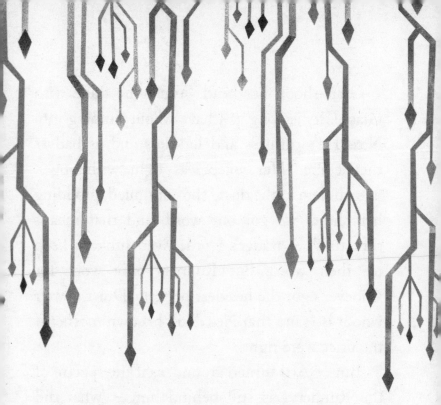

THE WORKSHOP

'What's going on, Gran?' Railey said, skidding to a stop inside an alley edged with brown, leggy cactuses.

Gran stopped so abruptly that Railey smacked right into the fluff of her cardigan.

'The Junkers sent a *Runner* after us,' she repeated, with a shake of her head. 'An' Nox too. The worst o' the lot of 'em.'

'Nox?'

Gran shook her head. 'You don't trade with Glass City as long as I have wi'out running into Nox. He's ruthless and lightless and as bad as they come.' Her voice was tight with anger. 'Down here in the dust,' she continued, prodding her chest, 'we got our word, and that means somethin'. A trader's word. Even Junker's keep ter their word, but Runners only work for whoever's got the heaviest pockets. Dun't matter who it is – and that Nox'd kill his own mother if the price were right!'

'But—' Atti turned around, as if the spectre of the Runner was still behind him – 'what did we do?'

'Nothing, yet,' Gran muttered.

'Yet?'

Gran started to hobble away again.

'Gran!'

'There's a war bubblin' up like someone shook up a great bottle of pop,' Gran shouted, flinging her arms in the air. 'Been fizzing up for longer than you been alive, and Izmae has been tryin' to unscrew the cap for years. Well, seems like she's done it. If they sent Nox after us then it must be soon – quick now.'

Gran pulled Railey into the darkness between two containerblock walls. The gap was so narrow she could feel the heat of the metal on her arms.

'Where are we going?' she panted.

'Home,' Gran muttered, almost invisible, even though she was only a few footsteps ahead. 'The secret way.'

Atti had scrambled up and was riding on the SmartGoggles propped in Railey's hair. His back ached from the crash and his head felt like it was still spinning through the air.

'Why do we need a secret way home, Gran?' he asked, already afraid of the answer.

'Ter keep you safe.'

'From Nox?' Atti asked, scampering on to Railey's shoulder. 'From the Junkers? What do they want with us? What haven't we done yet?'

Railey glanced down at the gecko. An uncomfortable thought nagged her. Nox was looking for a pilot. Had he seen Atti tumble out of the Fox when he'd crashed? Had he meant him? *Them?*

Gran turned a corner and the alley opened out a little.

'If Nox knows then *she* knows,' she muttered, tapping the walls as she passed and listening to the flat sound they made, 'and if *she* knows then we got no time left – but that's where my plans end and his begin.' She let out a sob. 'But rumour was he fell off a heap years back. So what's to do now then? What's to do?'

Railey could see the sweat glistening on Gran's forehead, and the sound of her footsteps was one-sided, like she was limping.

'How much further, Gran?'

'Nearly there, my love.'

Still tapping, Gran led them down a stony staircase and into a part of the city that Railey didn't recognize.

There were no homey orange lights here, just the blue dark of the desert night. The containerblocks here were packed so close you could jump between them, and the narrow streets were empty save for giant rust patches that swirled in the air like orange snowflakes.

'What *is* this place?' Railey said, holding out

her hand and catching a piece of rust in her palm.

'The oldest part of Boxville. As old as the Soup itself,' Gran said, tapping the rusting wall again and turning into another claustrophobic street.

'Why is it abandoned?' Atti asked.

'Steel only lasts so long in the desert before it gets the rot. They built the rest of the city up around these old blocks and closed 'em off. Only those of us with a few creases around our eyes remember it now.'

Atti jumped. A SteelSheep appeared from around a dark corner. It stopped when it spotted them and watched them pass by with its empty yellow eyes.

'Keep ter the edges,' Gran hissed. 'They got spies everywhere and in everything. Maybe that thing there's looking fer more than just metal tonight.'

The sheep ambled along the containerblock wall and joined others that were picking at pieces of a long-fallen neon sign.

Railey watched them. She couldn't help but wonder if the broken Fox had already met a similar fate. Munched to bits by sharp alloy teeth, or already in the ion-smelter, being melted down and reformed into a paperclip or a toilet roll holder for the people in Glass City.

Railey swallowed a sob. She couldn't bear the idea of her precious drone being turned into something so boring. So practical.

Gran tapped the wall again, and this time was met with a long ringing tone. 'Ah,' she said, 'here we are.'

She wiped away the flaky rust, revealing a narrow door cut roughly into the steel. A frothy tankard was scratched above it, with 'The Bag o' Nails' scrawled underneath.

Gran glanced left and right, then pushed the point of her multitool into the hidden lock.

They stepped inside and a tiny bell announced their presence to the deserted bar and empty tables.

Gran ambled over to the bar, tested the floor with her slippers, then stomped down hard. A hatch sprang open with a loud snap.

'Always been a bit lively, that . . .' Gran said, before disappearing down a dark, twisting staircase heavy with the wet, mouldy smell of the city's storm drains.

Railey followed Gran into the labyrinth of tunnels that ran beneath the city.

Gran always said she had too many secrets to live in an overcrowded containerblock where everyone could see your business. She preferred the dark quiet of the tunnels. Now Railey was beginning to understand why.

She didn't speak, just concentrated on the sound of Gran's splashing slippers until the twists and turns of tunnels became familiar, and she saw the warm glow of the workshop door up ahead.

The workshop was lit by a single pink neon sign that read 'Flamingo Club' in twisting script. Around it, salvaged parts hung on hooks and in bundles, waiting to make their way into the insides of a drone: wires twisted into coils and grouped according to colour and thickness; feathery fibreoptics; empty neon tubes; plugs needing sockets; sockets needing plugs; and circuit boards so old and heavy that even Railey couldn't see any real use for them.

A wooden workbench stretched across the far wall, hidden under the detritus of decades of rebuilds and trades and trouble. Above it, the wall was covered in shelves stacked with precariously balanced junk.

Railey breathed in the familiar smell of rust and solder, and felt her heart begin to slow.

Gran shuffled past her and collapsed into her chair in a puff of silvery dust.

Atti sprang down off Railey's shoulder and scampered along the workbench towards her.

'Gran?' he said, crawling on to her knee.

Her breath was coming out in fast little pumps. She held a shaking hand to her head and Railey saw there was blood on her knuckles. Her cardigan was torn and the knees of her overalls were covered in dirt – there were still bits of the raceway stuck in her cloudy hair.

'Railey, be a love . . .' she said, gesturing to the remade fridge in the corner of the room. Railey opened it and pulled out a foil packet with a pink sticker on the side.

'You're really not supposed to,' she said. 'The Doc said—'

'He'd have a lot more ter say about me fighting a Runner, I reckon,' Gran snapped, taking the pack and ripping off the top. She pulled out a fluffy cloud of pink glittery floss and stuck the whole thing into her mouth at once.

'Best medicine that,' she said, closing her eyes and sinking into the chair.

She chewed slowly for a while, a look of pure pleasure on her wrinkled face, then tears started to dribble from her closed eyes.

Atti crept up Gran's boiler suit and on to her chest.

He tapped her gently with a fat finger. 'It's OK, Gran—' he began, but he was cut off.

'It int OK!' Gran sobbed. 'It weren't ever going to be OK! What was I thinking? All these years . . .'

She looked at Atti, and her expression softened into a smile. 'Oh my little gecko,' she said, running a thumb over the crown of Atti's head, 'ter put yer in danger makes my heart hurt worse than anything. But what else could I do? There weren't any other way.'

Railey came over and held Gran's hand. 'You

have to tell us what's happening, Gran. Why are we in danger?'

Gran collapsed into another fit of sobs.

'I'd gi all the junk in the Soup ter make it different,' she sobbed. Railey didn't know what to say. She'd never seen Gran cry before. She put her soft hand against Railey's cheek and held it gently. 'Forgive me, my love.'

'It'll be OK, Gran—'

'No it won't!' she cried, snatching the hand back. 'He fell off a heap years back, and I done nothing – *nothing* to work out another plan.

'He trusted me ter sort it, with or without him,' she muttered. 'He knew the consequences. But I done my bit building it and keeping it safe, then I let me mind slip! And now if Nox knows, then she knows. And she won't sleep until she's got it!'

Railey and Atti looked at each other.

'Who's "she", Gran?' Railey said slowly. 'Is it . . . Izmae?' she added, remembering the name Gran had muttered in the alleyway when she was talking about a war.

Gran grabbed her sleeve. 'Never set foot in the

same Sphere as her, Railey. Promise me?'

'The Spheres?' Atti lifted his head. 'She's a Junker?'

Gran pursed her lips in disapproval. 'Oh, the worst of 'em! Her clan done things that would make yer blood boil. But Izmae's clever, cleverer than any other Junker I ever met, that's the problem. She's made herself a leader, or as close to a leader as Junkers'll allow.' Gran shook her head. 'I never wanted nothing ter do with her,' she groaned. 'Oh! But the universe had different ideas!' She looked at Railey and then started sobbing again. 'An' here I am, sending her right after you! But I had no choice, honest no. What else could I do?'

Gran looked at Railey in a way that made the hairs stand up on her arms.

'All me life I been a half, Railey, understand? Half trader, half Junker. Never wanted or accepted by either. To the Junkers I was half dirt, a horrible mistake. And down here in Boxville I was half Junker, and not to be trusted. Always a half, Railey – never a whole.'

She shook her head. 'And I dreamt of the

Spheres. Of getting out of this stinking hot city, shaking off the dust – nothing but sky above me and adventures ahead of me . . .'

Her voice faded.

'He promised me he'd take me up there, after it was done. Let me join them. Make me a whole,' she whispered to herself. 'And so I helped him. Because he weren't like the others – he was quiet and gentle, and that made me trust him, take him for his word. But that was before – before Izmae found out – and then, oh!'

Railey cradled Gran's head as she shook with heavy sobs.

Atti glanced at the workshop's old buckled door. If Nox had seen where they went he'd have caught up with them by now, and apart from the slow drip of water the tunnels outside were quiet.

'We'll sort it, Gran, we always do,' Railey said, stroking Gran's puffy hair. 'We're engineers, remember, and engineers don't see problems, we see plans.'

Atti huffed. 'Let me know when you have one, then,' he said, curling into a ball on Gran's knee. Railey made a face at him.

'I never meant for none of it,' Gran whispered, her voice fading.

'We know.'

Railey rocked Gran until her sobs turned to silence and finally, the soft snores of sleep. She sat silently, staring at the workshop wall. Her mind was racing. Going over the events of the last few hours. She felt as though she'd been flung out of real life straight into a nightmare.

What on earth was happening to them?

What had Gran done?

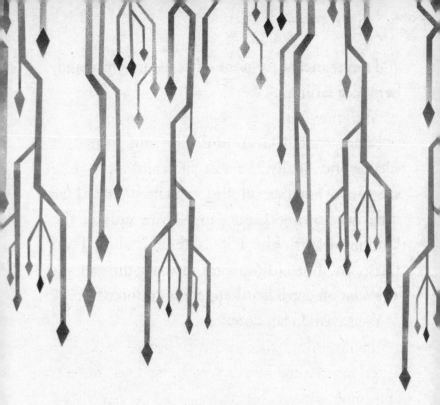

NOX

Atti shifted on Gran's knee. Something tickled his subconscious circuits, like an itch he couldn't scratch. Groggy with sleep, he opened one eye.

Railey was snoring gently, her lip twitching with bad dreams. Gran was still, other than the soft rise and fall of her chest.

The workshop's neon light hummed gently,

the tunnels outside were still, save for the steady *drip-drip* of tunnel water.

Still, that funny feeling tugged at him.

He opened his other eye.

Welt was staring at him. Flashing his plastic teeth in a horrible grin. He reached out to grab Atti, but a gloved hand slapped him away.

The gecko froze.

Bright, hot sparks were dancing around the tiny workshop, spitting from the armpit of a dark shape standing behind Welt.

'Hello, Pilot,' Nox said with a wide smile. He tilted his masked head to one side. 'I was expecting something . . . bigger.'

Atti leapt on to Railey. 'Nox!' he shouted. 'Nox!'

'What?' Railey fell off the arm of the chair.

Gran jolted awake. 'You!' she croaked.

Welt crouched by Railey's ear. 'Told yer I'd get to yer secret, din't I?' he said, gleefully.

Atti leapt off Railey's shoulder on to Nox's face. With an animal hiss, he dug his toes deep into the Runner's cheeks.

Nox reeled, clutching his face.

At the same time, Railey sprung up and ran for the door, pulling Gran along by the cardigan.

She pinballed between Welt and Nox, throwing her weight against them so they fell back into the overloaded workbench.

The impact shifted the delicate balance of junk on the shelf above, and the parts began to fall around them like rain. Nox, still clutching his face, didn't see the dumb-bell until it hit his masked head with a loud *crack*.

'Go!' Atti shouted, landing on Railey's shoulder. 'Quick!'

Railey turned to the door, but Welt was in her way.

'No! You ain't going *nowhere*, yer filthy *cheats*!'

Railey kicked him square in the stomach. 'Better a cheat than a *rat*,' she hissed. 'That's how bad you want the series, is it? Rather us dead than winning!'

Behind them, Nox groaned.

'Cheats is worse!' Welt coughed, clutching his stomach. 'That *thing* weren't even a drone – it was a ship with a pilot!' He pointed at Atti, his eyes red with rage. 'Now I'm gonna spend the rest of me days burning ter a crisp in them solar farms cos of you and that . . . *thing*!'

Blood rushed to Railey's cheeks. He was right. They *had* cheated, but it made her blood boil to think Welt would give them up to the Runner – cheats or not.

'I'm going to punch them teeth right out your mouth!' she said, moving forward, but Atti tugged on her ear.

'Less talking, more running!'

Out of the corner of her eye, Nox was starting to twitch.

Gran leant on her shoulder. Railey could feel her old bones shaking.

'Leave me,' she croaked. 'Get ter the Junk Market. You'll find help there.'

The Junk Market? No one in their right mind went looking for help there – and Gran clearly wasn't in her right mind.

Railey shook her head. 'No, Gran. C'mon.'

She ran as fast as Gran would let her through the dark tunnels of the city's storm drains, taking the most confusing route she could think of. But despite her efforts, the green beams of Nox's eye screens soon began to light up the dank tunnels in bright flashes.

'He's getting closer!' Atti shouted, clutching on to Railey's hair.

'The Tops, Railey!' Gran breathed in her ear.

'We can't go to the Junk Market, Gran. It'll be crawling with Junkers—'

'Yes,' Gran wheezed, 'the Junkers will help us.'

'But we're running *away* from Junkers, aren't we?' Atti said.

The Junk Market in the city's rooftops was notoriously dangerous. It was crawling with Junkers who would rather fight than talk – and had little time for anyone who spent their lives with their feet on the ground.

'There –' Gran said, as they whipped around another corner – 'up them stairs, little one – they'll do.'

Gran pointed to a rickety metal staircase that led up out of the tunnels. It was so rotten and rusty that it looked like a strong gust of wind would collapse it – but without a better plan, and with the ring of Nox's boots growing closer,

Railey launched them up.

They broke out of the clinging damp of the storm drains and into the grey-blue light of the early morning.

The old staircase clung to the side of the wonky containerblock with the tips of its fingers. It shook and creaked in protest as Railey and Gran scrambled up its rusty steps, past layers of irregular container houses either abandoned or shuttered tight against the wind.

Atti kept watch behind them from his perch on Railey's head – scanning the shadows for the shape of the Runner. It wasn't long before the staircase started to pound with his footsteps.

'Up, up, up!' Atti urged, pulling on Railey's hair like it would help.

Gran moaned. The higher they climbed, the harder she was to haul up the stairs. Her old hands shook on the railings and, as the air thinned and the drop became ever more nausea-inducing, her breath came in rapid and ragged wheezes. Eventually, finally, they made it past the dozens of layers of container homes and out on to the rooftop.

The air was cold, free from the heat of the steel containers and the clog of the desert dust. It whipped strands of Railey's hair across her cheeks and made her nose run.

Hidden around them, hundreds of huge silver air vents were coughing out the hot air from the streets far below, wrapping the rooftops in a thick blanket of steam.

Railey walked Gran to the edge of the roof, then stopped.

'Was' a matter?' Gran said breathlessly, collapsing on to the floor with a clink of tools and toecaps.

The steel walkway that linked the containerblock rooftops had long rusted away, leaving nothing but a steamy gap between them and escape on to the rooftops beyond.

'We can't cross,' Railey said. 'It's too far to jump. There's so much steam I can't even see if there's another rooftop to land on.'

Gran turned back to the stairwell. The black dot of the Runner was directly below them, circling up and up at speed.

'Can't go back down neither,' she said.

Railey cast about, looking for another way down, or something long and strong enough to bridge the gap – but, save for a cluster of vents in the middle, the containerblock roof was empty.

'Railey –' a pressure on her neck. Atti's soft, tiny hand – 'we need to go.'

'We can't jump it, Atti.'

A tug on her earlobe. 'We can.'

'What are you talking about?'

The wind was gusting now, whistling loudly between the metal stairs. It carried something else with it too – a stale, sour smell, like rotting bins.

The gecko pulled her chin towards him. 'If we don't go now, he'll *kill* us.' Their eyes met – hers bright green, his the endless sparkling blue of the night sky.

'If we do move, *that* will kill us,' she said, pointing at the misty rooftops.

'Not if you jump to the left.'

'What?'

'Just jump to the left. Trust me. My eyes see more than yours.'

Gran pulled herself to her feet with a deep

grunt and took off her slippers – they'd lost all their fur and the steel-toe-caps gleamed.

'Away with yer,' she said, turning towards the top of the stairs, where Nox was about to appear. 'Get away, fast as yer can.'

Railey's eyes went wide. 'What?'

Gran pulled her hand out of Railey's. Her black pebble eyes were hard. 'Fast as yer can, now. I won't hold him fer long.'

Railey could see the green beams of Nox's eye screens piercing the steam.

'The likes o' him never got the better of me before,' Gran muttered. 'I ain't about ter let it happen now. Railey. Atti. Go.'

When Railey didn't move, Gran grabbed her arms in a grip as strong as container steel.

'If he gets yer now it's all fer nothing. Understand? I dun my bit, now you got ter do yours—' Her voice faltered.

Railey opened her mouth, but her throat was too dry to speak. The look on Gran's face was scaring her much more than the Runner on the stairs.

Gran cupped Railey's cheek and stroked Atti's head.

'But,' Atti said, 'we don't know what to do.'

Gran turned back to the staircase. 'Find the Junkers. The chart makers,' she said. 'If yer lucky, they'll find you.'

'But Junkers—'

'GO!'

'No! Wait. Gran!'

Gran whipped around so fast all Railey saw was a blur. She felt a sharp shove on her shoulder and suddenly she was tumbling through thick pillows of mist. Gran had pushed her, making sure to aim her fall slightly to the left.

Gran watched them fall, then turned back slowly.

Nox was standing at the top of the stairs, sparks spraying from the dead metal arm by his side.

'They're gone,' she shouted, holding her slipper aloft.

Nox, unfazed by the threat of a steel-toe-cap, ran past her to the edge of the roof and let out a frustrated howl.

Gran ran back to the stairs. She summoned all her strength and brought her slipper down hard on the two eroded bolts that were the only things left holding them to the rooftop.

She shoved the rusted railing hard. The staircase shivered, then toppled away into the mist.

'There. No one's going anywhere fast now!' she said.

'No!' Nox spun back, PunchGun raised.

Gran winced, waiting . . . but the punch didn't come.

Gran opened her eyes.

'What's this, then?' she said. 'Why int you blasting me away?'

'You're really, really making me want to,' the Runner growled. 'But I don't see how that would help.'

'Help?' Gran was confused. 'When's a Runner ever been interested in helping anyone— *Oh!*'

The colour drained from Gran's face. Something heavy settled in the pit of her stomach.

'Runners dun't wait ter kill,' she said, shaking. 'If you wanted us dead, you'd have blasted us away right there at the raceway – but you din't.'

'No. I didn't,' Nox agreed.

Gran looked back into the mist where Railey and Atti had just disappeared.

'Spheres above!' she gasped. 'What have I done?'

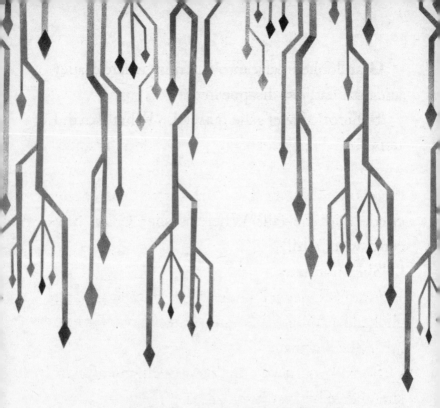

THE CASCADE

For a second, Railey was suspended in a blur of blue sky, orange rooftops and white mist – then her body hit something thicker and gloopier than water.

Green was all around – in her jacket, in her eyes, up her nose. It smelt rotten, like sweaty salad leaves, and there was the steady hum of pumps and filters.

'Gran!' She coughed as she resurfaced and struggled against the gluey water. 'Gran!'

The rooftop was gone, obscured by steam. She sank into the water again; her sodden trainers were dragging her down and she had to kick them off to get back to the surface. 'Atti!' she cried. 'Did she fall? Where is she? Gran! She can't swim. Atti!'

'She's not here.'

'Gran?' Railey fell under the surface again and choked back the sour, lumpy water. 'Look for her, Atti! She'll drown!'

'So will you if you don't stop struggling!' Atti shouted. 'This way. Kick hard.'

Railey swam through the goo and mist in the direction of Atti's voice. She groped blindly until she felt hard metal under her fingers. A surge of nausea hit her and she spat a mouthful of sour sludge back into the fetid water.

'What *is* this?'

'Algae farm,' the gecko said quietly. He was on the edge of the vat, looking through the steam at her with glossy eyes. 'I don't think he's following.'

'Did you see Gran fall?'

The gecko shook his head and walked out of sight. 'We've got to keep moving. There's another vat here. Follow me.'

'But – Atti!'

Railey heaved her algae-laden body over the ledge and gasped as she landed with a splash in another stinking pool.

She kicked to the side where a thick pipe dipped below the surface, creating bubbles that erupted all around her and smelt like morning breath when they burst. She heaved herself up and looked around the other pools – the algae water was still and quiet.

A great hole opened up in her chest.

Atti dipped over the edge of the vat and reappeared. 'Three more vats,' he said. 'The last one looks like oil.'

Finally, Railey emerged out of the algae farm like a swamp monster and landed in a heap on the hot metal of the containerblock rooftops. She let tears run down her cheeks, cleaning them of the goo.

'Gran . . .'

'We need to keep moving,' Atti said flatly. He was sitting a little ahead of her, his body pressed against the warm metal. He knew as well as she did that an old lady was unlikely to be able to stop someone like Nox for long, even one as fierce as Gran.

Railey pulled herself up. Her precious racer's jacket was heavy as lead with at least five different breeds of mutated, power-generating algae. Her jeans rubbed together, and her bare feet stuck to the hot, dry metal of the rooftops like they were covered in glue.

'C'mon.' Atti scampered in front of her, dipping in between the clustered boxes, checking the way was clear before she came stomping behind. The image of Railey, miserable and angry and covered in goo, would have been funny in any other circumstances. But Atti had lost his sense of humour.

Railey pulled the wet jacket out and let it slap against her back. She gave the gecko a withering look. 'I'm all stuck together.'

'Take the jacket off.'

Railey looked like he'd slapped her. 'I'll

pretend you didn't say that, lizard. This jacket is all we have now.'

She sounded angry, but Atti knew that anger was just Railey's way of coping. He left her be.

'Where are we even going?'

'I don't know.' Atti jumped over a pipe. 'Let's just keep going.'

'I can't just keep going. I can't.'

Atti turned around and found Railey standing still, chest heaving, doing her very best to stop herself from crying.

'Railey?'

'What's happening, Atti?' she asked, swallowing back a sob. 'I don't know what's happening. I never been so scared in all my life.'

Atti ran up her leg and on to her shoulder and placed a squidgy hand against her cheek. 'Let's find somewhere to rest a while.'

Railey nodded. Atti jumped off her shoulder and reappeared a few seconds later, pointing to the dark gap between two huge vents.

He gestured for Railey to follow.

'As good a spot as any.'

Railey collapsed into the gap with a squelch,

and tried to get her breath. She sat very still, focusing on the steady *chug, chug, chug* of the fans on either side of them.

A horrible feeling crept across her skin.

'Railey?'

She felt Atti's body wrap around the back of her neck. She didn't move for a long time. Panic chooses the quiet moments to get its grip on you.

She stared through the gap in the metal, feeling her anxiety growing and fizzing through her like a charge of electricity. It made her legs jump and her teeth chatter.

Atti curled up on the top of her knee. 'You're shaking.'

Railey didn't say anything.

The gecko sighed. 'It has been quite a night.'

Railey wrapped her arms around her legs.

'One minute she's right there, then the next she's . . . she's . . .'

'I know.'

Railey punched the side of the alcove.

'What's all this got to do with us anyway?!' she cried, suddenly angry. 'If Gran's right, if there is a war, then what can we do about it? A girl and a tiny little gecko? It must be her marbles, Atti. She was making it up.'

'Nox wasn't made up,' Atti said, gazing at the drifting clouds through the gap. They were starting to thin as the night finally gave way to early morning. 'So there must be something.'

'And that horrible scorpion, Welt!' Railey's hands were balled into shaking fists by her sides. 'If I ever find myself breathing the same air as that slippery sand snake again I'm going to make sure he rots in them solar farms. I'll drag him there myself, and I'll crush that stupid fancy drone of his too . . . I'll—'

She stopped at the gentle pressure on her neck. 'Welt's mad because we're cheats, that's all.'

Railey's shoulders slumped. Atti was right. Welt *was* the best drone flyer.

Gran had been obsessed with the races, with the designs for the drone – urging Atti to win, helping Railey tweak the Fox until it was more agile than a sandfly. Railey had been so swept up in Gran's enthusiasm for the races that she'd pushed the fact they were cheating into the back of her mind. It had become so normal to her that it had stopped feeling wrong. It felt wrong now, and strange, and for the first time she wondered why.

Thanks to Nox, she'd never know. She wiped her eyes with her grubby sleeve. 'What are we going to do?' she said.

Atti pushed his snout against the tip of her nose.

'Let's think. Plans not problems, remember?'

Railey nodded and tried to focus her panicking brain back on to a more logical path.

'Nox is still looking for us, no matter what we want to believe—' the gecko said, twisting his tail nervously.

Railey nodded. '—and he's not going to stop, neither. And he knows about the workshop, so there's no way we can go home.'

'Would anyone help us?' Atti suggested. 'The old traders? Gran's friends?'

Her mind spun through the people Gran had considered friends. It didn't take long. Gran had lost most her friends when she'd lost her marbles.

She shook her head.

'Someone in Glass City?'

Railey huffed and glanced through the gap at the distant towers that stuck out from behind the mountains like shards of glass – hence the name.

'Glass City people don't help Boxville people,' she said. 'You know that.'

The city visible beyond the mountains was a sprawling, modern metropolis, clean and gleaming, filled with grand boulevards and lush, green parks.

Boxville had once been Glass City's rubbish pit, vast and stinking, until people who disagreed with the city's wasteful ways came out and began to turn it into a city of its own – one built out of the scraps the well-to-do left behind, the people of Boxville making their living out of remaking Glass City's rubbish.

Railey sighed. The twin cities were separated only by a low ridge of mountains, but might as well have been worlds apart.

Up in their glistening towers, the people of Glass City tried their best to forget that Boxville, and Earth's rubbish problem, existed. Gran even said they built their towers so the windows faced the other way.

No. They wouldn't find help from anyone there.

Railey put her head in her hands.

'If Welt's blabbed to the other racers about us cheating, then they're not going to help. They'll hate me.'

'So, we can't go back.'

Railey shook her head. 'Looks like we're stuck, then,' she said. 'Might as well just stick it out here until the sun comes up and cooks us up like a couple of hot potatoes.'

Atti watched the clouds. The kilometres of rooftops were appearing between them now; he could see the silvery glint of the ventilation pipes in the sunlight.

'We do have somewhere to go,' he said, picking his words carefully. 'We do have a plan, of sorts.'

Railey looked at him. The gecko shrugged.

'You've lost it, Atti. I'm not going to the Junk Market.'

The gecko gave her one of those looks that made her blood boil.

'Gran told us to go there.'

'Last week she told me I was her Uncle

Neville, Atti.' She shook her head. 'Gran's brain's as wonky as a containerblock, you know that—'

'Not about this. You know it.'

Railey chewed her hair. Infuriatingly, she knew the gecko was right. Something had stirred in Gran when she'd seen Nox at the arena. Something that had given her old body the strength to fight and run like she was thirty years younger than she was.

Atti watched the change in her expression and nodded. 'So. We go to the market and we wait to be found.'

Inside her sticky jacket, Railey shivered.

'I don't like not knowing, Atti. I like to understand the workings of things. This has my head in a spin.'

'And that's why we have to go and find out what's what. As soon as the sun's up, OK?'

Railey let out a long resigned breath and leant over to examine her filthy bare feet. No one in the Junk Market was going to take her seriously with her toes showing.

Suddenly, a bright flash lit up the rooftops around them all the way to the dusty mountains on the horizon, and the gleaming towers of Glass City beyond.

'Oh look,' said Atti. 'The Cascade is starting.'

Below them, the great city of Boxville hushed, as if a blanket had been thrown over it.

The second flash was a big one. Directly in front of them, beside the bright line of the crescent moon. A third followed, lower in the sky, yellower and lasting long enough to make an arc across the inky blue.

A scatter of bright white dots glimmered in the east, followed by a spray of deep purple and a flash-bang of green.

The Cascade was beautiful, but it was deadly. The people of both cities watched it like a ritual, in awe of its majesty but with knots in their stomachs.

Railey put her hand in her pocket and pulled out a smooth lump of melted metal. It was objects like this that she was watching right now. High above their heads, in the sapphire-blue pocket between the sky and space they called the Spheres, a thousand Junkers were busy scrapping the millions of bits of space debris that fell out of orbit around Earth – tearing it up, extracting the bits they could sell and then sending the rest down to burn up in the Earth's mesosphere.

'Iron,' Railey whispered as a yellow flash streaked comet-like to the west, imagining a mangled engine part crashing through the air. Railey knew from hours spent in the workshop that the colours of the Cascade were created by different types of junk: iron was yellow; blue for copper; aluminium was bright, flashing white.

Funny really, that it was all just rubbish.

At the beginning of the twenty-first century, Earth was overrun with waste. So the rich countries paid the poorer ones to take their waste away, to dismantle their ships and old computers and plastic bags, and bury them in great holes in the ground. But the poor countries became rich themselves, they had their own ships and old computers and plastic bags to get rid of, and quickly, the planet ran out of room.

So the powerful families that ran Glass City decided to push their rubbish out into the sky instead, and space became the new, endless, hole in the ground. The Soup was born – a ring of speeding rubbish orbiting around the Earth, so thick in places that it sometimes clouded out the stars.

And with the Soup, came the Cascade.

Everything that goes up must come down, and soon, larger bits of junk and debris began to fall out of orbit in the Soup back towards the surface, smashing into the cities below with the force of bombs.

The families that ran Glass City and created the Soup were banished to the sky, told to scrap the junk in the mesosphere so it never hit the city again – they became the Junkers, and up there in the dark, they prospered.

Everyone in Boxville knew they should be grateful for the Junkers – the Cascade had become less deadly since the clans had started to pull rubbish from the sky – but life in the Spheres had made the Junkers tough and fierce. They hated life on the ground, and only ever came down to solid ground to trade and cause trouble.

Railey sighed. Today, as soon as the sun came up, they were going to walk right into a market full of them.

Railey felt her eyelids going heavy. She saw two more sparks of light (the deep orange of sodium, and bright violet of potassium) before she fell into a fidgety, uncomfortable sleep.

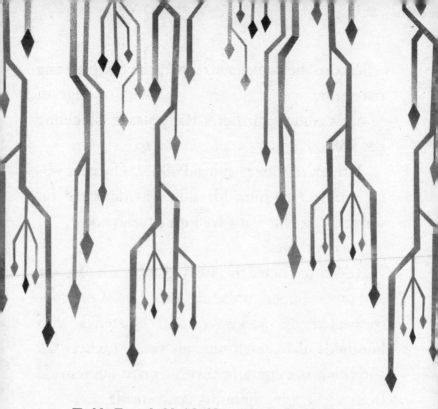

THE JUNK MARKET

Railey ran the sleeve of her jacket along her sweaty forehead, leaving a glistening snail trail on the patched leather. They'd been walking for less than an hour, but already she could feel her skin turning pink and her tongue becoming as dry and prickly as a cactus.

The Junk Market was held during the day – while the rest of Boxville slept away the heat

– because the Junkers scrapped the Soup during the night.

'How much further?' Railey said, shielding her eyes.

Atti ran in a zigzag ahead of her. The heat was no problem to him; his skin was designed for weather like this – it gave him a turbo boost.

'Nearly there.'

Ahead of them, the rusty patchwork of roofs and pipes dipped, revealing a section of rooftops connected by walkways, and clustered with hundreds of huge chrome air vents, each as tall and thick as a container, with a giant fan remade from a jet engine spinning lazily inside.

Around them, the Junk Market heaved with people and scrap and steam and rippling heat.

Railey heard a buzzing above them and looked up. The air above the market was swarming with drones.

'Look, Atti. Drones.'

'Not drones,' Atti said, focusing his enhanced eyes on the dots. 'They're gyros. Human-sized.'

The gyros were remade from old motorbikes and jet skis, with large helicopter rotors attached to the top. They swooped and dived in the air above the market, dragging trailers heavily laden with goods for trade.

Railey pulled her collar close around her ears and entered the market with Atti perched on her shoulder, his blue galaxy eyes wide in wonder.

She worried about the way he acted – showing off the obvious intelligence behind those dark, mesmerizing eyes. Atti had abandoned the act of playing the dumb desert lizard. This was the Junk Market after all – there would be wares on display here more precious than a mechanical pet. But Railey thought of Nox's words and wondered if they were being too reckless.

The thought was fleeting. As she walked closer, the size and spectacle of the Junk Market solidified into reality around them: she'd never seen anything like it in her life.

Radiation clickers attached to stalls chirruped like songbirds as the colourful occupants of the mesosphere stomped back and forth, the weight of their goods and magnetic boots making the containerblock rooftops groan and sag.

The junk traders had their stalls tucked into

the shadows of the huge ventilation ducts, protected from the sun by flapping awnings.

Beneath the awnings, the whole of the Soup seemed to be spread out for all to see – there were stalls selling components so small they caught the sun like silver glitter, while others were piled with junk bigger than anything Railey had ever seen – cars and helicopters and small planes, still whole, stacked four high, next to towers of twisted, broken machinery.

As Railey wandered between the first row of stalls she licked her lips, thinking of the things she could make just from the parts spread out directly in front of her filthy bare feet.

The Junkers that milled around them came in assorted varieties too – some had long hair braided with wire cables, others wore sunbleached plastics strung into necklaces, some wore a kind of armour remade from old scraps of melted metal.

They all bore the signs of a life lived hard. Most were scarred, some were missing limbs, others had their bodies retrofitted with remade parts that made Welt's Scrabble teeth look subtle.

It hit her then, sharp and hard as a nail gun – this was Gran's old life spread before them. There were people she knew here, before her mind began to wander. All the stories, all the old junk in the workshop, the boiler suit she wore every day of her life – it all came from here.

And now it was all gone.

An intense loneliness gripped her. Her knees went weak. She stumbled, steadying herself on the edge of the nearest stall.

She took a few deep breaths and then saw that, with a luck that had evaded them until now, the stall was selling boots.

They were made of thick rubber fixed together with complicated straps, and had a thick metal sole. Each pair looked way too big for her, but Railey started to pick through the pile anyway, hoping to find something smaller and more normal-looking underneath.

'Never seen a gecko that colour before,' someone said.

Railey jumped. A boy about her age was standing at the other end of the stall. He was shorter than her, and looked like he was covered head to toe in thick orange rust, but it was just that his skin and hair were that exact colour.

'Your pet,' he said, nodding at Atti.

Railey felt Atti bristle. He hated being called a pet.

'Yellow geckos are as common as SteelSheep in Boxville,' she said quickly.

'You should be careful,' the boy said, looking at her strangely. 'There's Junkers here that would kill to get their hands on it.'

The boy held her gaze for a second, then went back to examining the object in his hands.

Railey pushed Atti into her collar, and rubbed her palms on her jeans. She was sweating, and it had nothing to do with the heat of the sun.

The boy was holding a shiny box, and was fiddling with a giant antenna poking out of the top.

'Castbox,' he said, following Railey's gaze. 'It lets you hijack TV signals. My dad used to have one just like this. Didn't think I'd see one again.'

'No one's watched TV for a hundred years,' Railey said, picking through the boots ranged at the front of the stall.

'Maybe that's why, then,' the boy said, putting the box in his pocket. 'You should try these.'

He held a pair of blue rubbery boots out to Railey.

Railey frowned. They were obviously several sizes too large. Besides, how was she going to pay for them?

'They're MagBoots,' the boy explained. 'They look big, but they move to fit your feet.' He waggled one of the boots insistently. 'Try it.'

Railey took the boot and mumbled her thanks. When she pulled it on, the boot buzzed and the straps pulled in to fit the contours of her foot perfectly. Her eyes widened.

'First time in the Junk Market?' he said, picking up a helmet with a huge crack running down the visor and tossing it between his hands.

Railey nodded. 'Good to know it's that obvious.'

He looked at her feet. 'You're not exactly dressed for the Spheres. You stand out a bit. Fit OK?'

Railey stomped around, glad of the distraction. The boot did fit – perfectly. It felt lighter than her stinky old trainer had, too light for a chunky boot, but she guessed the magnets hidden in the soles had something to do with that.

'Like a glove, yeah.' She glanced at the boy, then at the stallholder, who was busy arguing about some flame-retardant gloves with a Junker as tall as the awning. She didn't have enough in her racing jacket to pay for a pair of MagBoots. Could she just walk away in them? Would the boy tell on her if she did? Would Gran ever forgive them for breaking the Traders' Code and stealing? Did she even have a choice?

The boy took the cracked helmet up to the stallholder. Carefully, Railey pulled the other boot on.

'If you're going to go, go *now*,' Atti whispered out of the corner of his snout.

Railey turned, heart pounding, ready to run, then felt a tap on her shoulder.

A giant Junker with a bright pink Mohawk was looking down at her.

'Hello there, dirt rat,' he said.

The heavy scar that ran across his chin pulled

as he smiled. His eyes moved from Railey to Atti, who was peeking out of her collar.

'You got a real cheek bringing it here, girl,' he said, lifting a huge wrench. 'Now, give it to me.'

Railey looked around her – no one in the market paid them any attention. She looked for the boy, but he'd disappeared.

Railey stepped back, knocking into the stall, sending the stack of MagBoots tumbling down around them.

The Junker held out his hand; two of his fingers were missing. 'Give it— Oi!' he cried as Railey turned, leap-frogged over the stall and disappeared into the crowds on the other side.

'Thief!' the stallholder shouted. 'She 'ent paid fer them boots!'

'Get that thieving dirt rat!' Mohawk cried, leaping over the stall and giving chase.

As Railey ran, she felt the Junkers in the crowd grabbing at her racer's jacket, but she twisted and ducked and skidded through them like a drunken trader on race day.

'What are you doing?' Atti cried in her ear. 'You're running around like a sandfly!'

'It's the boots!' she panted. 'I can't feel the ground!' The magnets in the soles were repelling the metal rooftops, making it impossible to put her feet down properly.

She stumbled again and fell hard on the hot metal.

'Get up, Railey!' Atti tugged her ear.

Railey felt someone pull her up by the jacket. She looked up. It was the blonde girl from the arena, the one who'd commented on Atti. This time a welding mask was pushed up on her head, holding the hair off her face, and Railey could see she was young, nine years old at the most.

'Hello again,' she said with a wicked grin, then kicked the back of Railey's boots. They hummed and stuck to the ground.

'You had them on the low-gravity setting,' she said, like Railey knew what that meant.

Behind them, Mohawk was pushing through the crowds towards them, wrench held high. Other Junkers had joined him now, all bashing their way through the crowd with mallets and bats.

The girl let go of Railey's jacket. 'This way,' she said, and ran away into the crowd.

Railey scrambled after her, moving faster now she could feel the ground.

'Why are you following *her*?' Atti cried.

'It's the girl from the arena,' she panted. 'Can't be a coincidence!'

Atti had to cling on to Railey's hair to stop himself falling out of her collar as she wove and ducked through the crowd after the smaller girl. 'Well, you should consult your passengers before running into danger!'

Railey pointed back to Mohawk. 'I'm running *away* from danger— Argh!'

A sudden blast of air knocked Railey, the girl and half the crowd around them to the ground. When she got back up she saw a flash of black behind Mohawk.

'Oh no!' Railey cried. 'It's Nox!'

'Who?' The girl was up on her feet and already pulling Railey along with her.

'The Runner from the raceway!'

The girl glanced over her shoulder. 'Oh, yeah.' She ducked between the legs of two tall Junkers hauling part of a children's playground on their backs.

'Quick!' she cried, leaving Railey in the dust behind her.

Running in the smaller girl's slipstream, Railey bounced through the market from lamp post to arcade machine to Junker to car bonnet. The girl kept glancing back with flicks of her huge eyes. Despite the smile, she looked terrified.

Atti crawled out on to Railey's shoulder. He looked back, using his computer eyes to keep track of the people chasing them.

Mohawk was closer now, and Atti could see the anger on his face as he tore between the unsuspecting traders, all the while ducking punches thrown from Nox's gun.

'Why are they both chasing us?' he cried.

'He's chasing *him*,' the girl shouted. 'Because *he's* chasing *us*.'

'And who are *you*?'

The girl swerved to the right, pushing them through a cluster of stalls selling huge rubber tyres. Railey followed, her lungs burning.

'After me!' the girl shouted, using the tyres as steps, jumping up the pile and landing with a thud on the top of the huge round ventilation shafts that housed the market stalls. 'Quick!'

Railey felt a sticky sensation in her boots as they recalibrated for use on the vents' sleek curved surface.

The girl pulled her forward again. 'Good job the boots know what they're doing.'

They bounced along from vent to vent. Mohawk and the other Junkers followed – still some way behind – but Nox didn't have boots with magnetic soles. He pushed through stalls below, one eye screen focused on them, the other on the market in front of him.

They jumped and jumped until the market stopped, and there was nothing but flat rooftops ahead.

They jumped down and stopped in front of a great gap in the rooftops. A black metal chasm, leading straight down to the dusty city streets below.

Railey's stomach flipped. The girl pulled her welding mask over her face and dragged Gran's SmartGoggles over Railey's eyes.

'Ready?' she said, as if they were about to do something they'd done a million times before.

Railey looked at the gap. It was a container wide at the most, and a warm wind blew up from the hot streets hidden in the darkness far below.

'That's a gap between containerblocks,' Railey panted. 'It'll be a kilometre deep!'

The girl ducked down and tapped a switch at the back of Railey's boots twice. 'Yeah, I know.'

She stepped casually forward, grabbed the front of Railey's jacket and pulled them both into the abyss.

Railey felt like her stomach had been wrenched out of her body through her throat. The vast containerblocks rushed past her in a blur of brown and blue. The wind rippled her face, forcing her mouth and eyes shut. She couldn't see. She couldn't breathe. All she could feel was the cold of the girl's hand in hers.

This was it. They were going to die.

The girl's hands moved to her arms, gripping them tight. She felt a pull in her feet, forcing her body flat against the air.

She opened her eyes a little and saw the girl floating in front of her, lying horizontal. Her MagBoots were stuck out towards the containerblock walls, the soles flickering green.

The girl gritted her teeth, tensing her body against the flow of the air and holding Railey's arms so hard it felt like she'd break her bones.

But, to her surprise, Railey felt them begin to slow.

Getting the idea, Railey urged her shaking legs out further behind her. As soon as she did, she felt the string of ultra-strong magnets in the soles of her boots attract to the containerblock's towering metal walls.

From inside her collar, Atti's enhanced ears began to pick up the soft *chukka chukka* of fan blades.

He pulled his head out just as a gyro swooped in a low arc past them and disappeared into the dark below.

The pilot brought the craft up under them slowly, so the girl could reach out and grab the metal trailer tethered to the back.

Railey landed with a thud, sending Atti cartwheeling out on to the hard metal, and the rest of the world thundering back to her.

The containerblocks were whizzing past them

in the opposite direction – balconies and windows and walkways visible now, some with curious faces peering out from the shadows.

Railey sat in the trailer, panting, trying to piece together what had just happened. 'Here!' A shout came from the pilot, who threw a helmet in her direction. 'Air's going to get thin pretty soon.'

Railey pulled the old helmet over her head – it had a huge crack along the length of the visor. Just like the one . . .

Her breath caught.

She peered around the crack at the pilot sat in the Harley-Davidson motorbike that made up the front of the gyro. His face was covered by a remade gas mask, but the rust-coloured hair was unmistakable.

The boy from the market.

The gyro tipped sharply upwards and the edges of the city were replaced by a dome of endless blue.

Railey looked across the trailer to where the girl was picking dirt out of her nails with the end of a knife.

What were these Junkers up to?

Atti tapped her neck and pointed to something in the sky ahead of them. It was dark and jumbled and impossibly big – like someone had picked up part of Boxville and launched it into the sky.

Railey pulled herself to the edge of the trailer to get a better look.

There was a long central platform surrounded by hexagonal decks clustered around four fat turrets topped with spinning rotors. The decks were covered with hundreds of jagged piles, like smaller versions of the Boxville containerblocks.

A Sphereship.

'HOVERSPORT' was painted in faded red letters on the side of the ship's huge central platform. All Sphereships were remade from old ocean-going ships – oil tankers and cruise ships for the most part. This one looked like it had once been a colossal rubber-skirted hovercraft, made even larger with added platforms and towers designed for holding the junk scrapped from the Soup.

Blood rushed in Railey's ears, and darkness

began to creep into the edges of her vision. They were so high. She blinked hard, fighting to stay awake.

She glanced at the boy, still focused on flying; and the girl, absorbed with picking her nails.

The last thing she thought was, *These two Junkers must have planned this all along*.

And then the world went black.

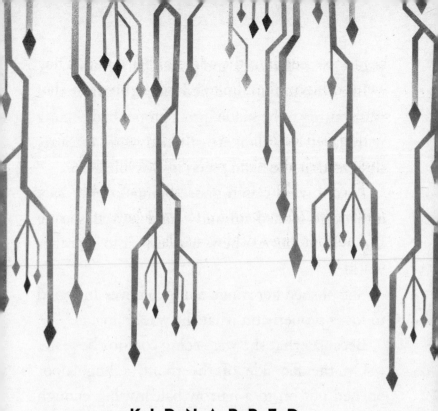

KIDNAPPED

Railey felt like someone had drilled the eyes out of her head. She tried to move but the pain throbbed harder the more awake she became.

'Atti?' Her voice sounded like the creak of a container door.

She felt up to her collar and found that she wasn't wearing her racing jacket. With a stab of panic, she rolled over and pulled herself up.

She'd woken up on a bed – or a mattress that was waiting to be made into a proper bed – slung with layers of blankets stitched with intricate designs that she hadn't seen in Boxville before.

A cool wind raised goose bumps on her bare arms. She looked up and found herself staring through a huge open window into another world.

She pushed her fringe out of her eyes and tried to focus properly on what she was seeing.

Because what she was seeing couldn't be real.

On the far side of the room, a huge door opened out on to a narrow balcony, big enough for a couple of chairs and a small table remade out of an old computer monitor.

Beyond the thin rungs of the balcony railing, cotton-wool clouds drifted between the peaks of tall, spiky mountains that stretched as far as Railey could see in every direction.

A glistening river flowed calmly between them, shining silver in the clear morning light. But there were no rivers near Boxville; and the mountains that separated them from Glass City were short and squat and covered in giant solar sails.

Then the horrible memory of Mohawk and Nox and the market and plunging between the containerblocks came rushing back to her.

Railey wasn't looking at mountain peaks, she was looking at great piles of junk. The 'river' that flowed between them, glistening like water in the sun, was a series of metal paths winding their way between them.

'Atti . . .'

The floor vibrated softly under her fingers – the deep rumbling hum of impossibly large engines turning somewhere below.

The Sphereship. She was on a Sphereship.

'Atti?'

Nothing. Just the hum of the deck and the soft clink of metal blowing in the breeze.

'Atti?'

She wobbled to her feet and turned her attention to the inside of the room.

The first thing she noticed was that its rusted metal walls were lined with delicately drawn charts: rolls and rolls of precious paper, dotted with strange shapes and measurements. Fine handwriting annotated each object: *NASA Bio Lab*, one read, *late 21st, elliptical orbit*.

Double-Decker Bus: intact but erratic orbit, said another. Another was annotated in red: *Rocket Fuel Tank, Unknown – DANGEROUS, still tracking*. Railey ran her fingers along them. This much paper would be worth a container or two in the city. She thought about putting some in her pockets, then remembered her jacket was gone.

On the far side of the room, a staircase remade from a red plastic children's slide wound up through the floor, and disappeared into another room above.

She padded around the opening and looked up – in the room above, the sun was casting sharp diamond shapes across curved walls. She heard the distant scrape of boots on metal coming from the room below.

She hesitated on the stair, then caught sight of something hanging above a scorched filing cabinet.

Relief flooded her body.

She pulled her racing jacket so hard that the hook jumped off the wall. Railey caught it before it reached the ground and made a noise, and pulled the jacket over her cold shoulders and gently felt the pockets.

'Ow.' She pulled her finger back and sucked the blood on the end. Atti's head appeared out of the top pocket, one eye open, the other closed.

'You OK?' she whispered, pointing to the room below. Voices had begun to drift up the stairs.

The gecko uncurled from her pocket and crept up on to her shoulder.

'It's a Sphereship, Railey . . .' he hissed right into her ear. 'We're on a Sphereship in the middle of the sky, and it must be *crawling* with Junkers.'

He curled his tail around him like a toddler holding a blanket.

Railey sat down on the edge of the steps and tried to listen to the voices.

Atti ran down on to her knee. 'Railey—'

'You're just panicking, Atti,' she said, trying to concentrate, 'and panicking never helped no one.'

The gecko pulled on his tail nervously. 'But what about all the chasing and fighting and, and . . . murdering.' His eyes were darting around the room like he expected to be ambushed any second.

Railey's stomach twisted. 'Stop it, Atti.'

The gecko didn't stop. His voice just got faster and higher.

'Junkers chop bits of each other off for fun, Railey. And they hate anyone that lives on the ground, which we do, or did, and oh, yes that's it, they KIDNAPPED us—'

Railey dismissed him. 'I know all that.'

'Then why aren't you panicking?!'

Railey shrugged. In truth, she was panicking so much it was making her heart shake, but telling Atti that wasn't going to help anyone.

'Gran never panicked, did she? Panicking isn't going to get us out of here.'

'Maybe she would be now, Railey, if she hadn't . . . if she wasn't— Oh!'

Atti jumped. His whole tail was now hanging from his outstretched hand – detached from his body.

'Atti!' Railey gasped.

The gecko's eyes went as round as rivets. 'Well, that smarts a bit.'

He winced and turned around slowly. 'How bad is it?'

Railey leant forward and peered at the disc of peachy flesh at the base of his back.

'Don't touch it!'

Railey shrugged. 'I don't know. How's it supposed to look?'

'Does it look weird?'

'Well, yeah, course it does.'

'Oh, thanks very much!' Atti turned back around and crossed his arms again, making the detached tail wobble in his grip.

The gecko winced. Atti's insides were made from computer parts, but his body was still gecko; tail dropping was normal, and it would grow back eventually, but it was still sore.

Railey shook her head.

'Look what they done to you.'

She fought the urge to pick up the gecko and pull him towards her. He hated being manhandled. But as he stood there on her knee, cradling his fallen tail like a comfort blanket, he looked so small and soft and breakable it made Railey's body ache.

'Stop it,' he said without turning back. 'Whatever it is you're thinking, stop it.'

Railey wiped her eyes. 'Get over yourself, you greasy little reptile.'

'Shush.' Atti pushed his squidgy hand against her lips, his head cocked to one side, listening to something that couldn't reach human ears.

'Can you hear what they're saying?'

'Shush!'

He jumped on to the stairs and gestured for Railey to get down on to the floor. She did, hanging her head over the opening just enough to remain unseen.

'. . . it's a mistake,' a strange electronic voice said. 'It has to be.'

Atti's eyes grew wide. Railey shuffled further forward on her stomach, so her head hung low enough to see into the room below.

It was a workshop, but nothing like the one Gran had carved deep in the belly of Boxville – this was light and cold and neat, with three walls lined with tools and a huge opening, through which Railey could see a dusty clearing surrounded by the bases of the junk mountains.

The girl from the market was sprawled out on a tatty Chesterfield armchair, drumming her dangling MagBoots against its side. Beside her was one of the strangest things Railey had ever seen.

A tablet screen – similar to the one Railey used when she pretended to pilot the Fox – was roving around the workshop on a set of caterpillar tracks, like a tiny tank. The screen was mounted on a long pole with pincer arms attached and was moving up and down and side to side like it was looking for something.

'Nox was chasing them, and Izmae's clan too.' Railey recognized the voice of the boy from the market, coming from a part of the room Railey couldn't see.

'But a girl and a gecko?' The computer's screen was flicking through a series of blank colours – grey, taupe, silver, then black. '*That's* the Pilot?'

Railey frowned. *The Pilot*? Nox was looking for a pilot too. She looked at Atti – did they really mean him?

'I was disappointed too, Tring,' the girl said with a roll of her eyes.

The boy walked into view, a layer of glittering metal dust covering him head to toe. He dumped a bag of shiny nuts and bolts on the workbench. 'I know. It doesn't make a lot of sense.'

The computer shook its screen. 'Do they have a ship?'

'If they did, they weren't using it – Care, you take the nuts, I'll sort the bolts.'

The girl, Care, leapt up from the chair and started to sort the salvaged nuts into sizes at amazing speed. 'Well I don't think they can do it,' she said. 'Because without me they wouldn't have even got out of the Junk Market. Razor was chasing us with half of Izmae's clan, and he was *angry.*'

Tring's screen turned green. 'Oh dear.'

'Yep,' Care said, not looking up from her work. 'We're all *dooooomed.*'

Railey twisted and arched her back, trying to get a better look at them. 'Razor must be the guy with the mohawk,' she whispered to Atti.

'Get back, Railey, they'll see you,' Atti hissed back.

She pushed the gecko off her face. 'No they won't.'

'They will. You're too big and loud – get back.' He stuck his toe in her nostril and pushed hard. 'I'll tell you what happens.'

'Ow! Atti! Stop it. Stupid wall maggot.' She pushed him away.

The gecko clung on. 'No, Railey. *Get back*, you sweaty skin bag!'

'Get off me, Atti! ATTI!'

Atti pulled Railey's hair with such force she hit her head on the upper edge of the slide. Losing her balance for just a moment, she tumbled down the steps and landed in a heap on the floor of the room below.

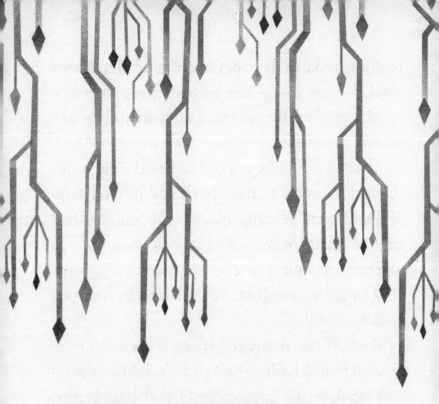

THE *HOVERSPORT*

When she opened her eyes, the tablet screen was above her head glowing a concerned orange.

The girl's head popped up beside it. 'I told you we were all doomed.'

The screen turned a deep, worried blue and pulled away.

Railey scrambled to her feet and held out her

multitool like it was a PunchGun. Her knees were shaking inside her jeans, but she kept her head high, just like she did in Boxville. People took advantage when they saw weakness, and Railey had gotten very good at pretending to be strong.

'Don't you get any closer,' she said in her fiercest trading voice.

The girl looked at the multitool. 'What are you going to do, file us to death? Oh nooooo, have mercy!'

'Care.' The computer flashed cactus green. The girl stuck her tongue out at it.

The closer Railey got to Care, the sicker she looked; her skin seemed transparent and her eyes were bright but sunken. She was as thin as a desert vine, too.

'It's rude to stare.'

Railey looked away. 'Sorry.'

'You will be.'

Railey bristled – she never let anyone talk to her like that in Boxville. She wasn't going to let it happen here either.

'A mouth like that would get you killed in

Boxville,' she growled, stepping forward.

Then a gecko foot jabbed her sharply in her neck, '*Your* mouth is going to get us killed at this rate, Railey!'

'Nobody's getting killed,' the boy said, 'not today anyway.'

Railey dropped the multitool to her side.

'Why did you kidnap us?'

'Rescued,' the boy said. 'When you're being chased by a Runner and half the junking clans from the northern hemisphere, the correct term is rescued.'

'Well – I . . .' The words dried up in Railey's mouth.

An awkward silence descended. Care chewed her lip. The computer looked at the boy, but he just continued to sort the bolts like there was no one else in the room.

Atti pulled up on to his haunches on top of Railey's head. 'Can someone please tell us what's going on?' he said.

Railey's eyes widened. He was talking in front of people! Then she remembered the strangeness of the situation and realized it probably didn't matter any more.

The smile dropped from Care's face. 'But, *you're* supposed to tell *us* what's going on,' she said, glancing at the boy, who'd stopped sorting. 'That's the plan.'

Railey blinked. 'The plan?'

Atti chewed his fat toe. 'What plan?'

The silence was deafening.

'You don't know anything?' Tring said, finally, moving away from the boy towards them.

Railey shrugged.

The Junkers looked at each other. The boy still hadn't moved.

Care's mouth was hanging open. 'Oh, no. Laurie, they really think they're drone racers.'

Railey flushed. 'We *are* drone racers. The best in the city, or we could have been before – before . . .' She couldn't finish the sentence. She couldn't say out loud what had happened to Gran, because it felt like saying it out loud would make it real.

The boy, Laurie, slammed the bolts down on the workbench.

'You're lying,' he said. 'Why are you lying? You

don't have to do that. We just saved you from Izmae's clan. We're on your side.'

His nostrils were flaring the way Railey's did when she was about to lose it, and his filthy hand was hovering over a wrench in his tool belt that was as long as his thigh.

Railey squared her shoulders.

She was confident she could fight him – he was a couple of years older than her, she reckoned, but he was small and slight. The wrench was a problem, though.

'I think everyone needs to just calm down,' Tring said, turning blush pink.

'Maybe you need to do some explaining to us first,' Railey growled, refusing to take her eyes off the boy. 'Maybe if we knew where we were and who we were with, then things might make more sense?'

Laurie's shoulders fell a little. He sighed. Now Railey was close enough she could see he looked tired, like the weight of the world was on his shoulders.

'I'm Laurie,' he said. 'You've met Care—'

'A pleasure.'

'Shush, Atti.'

'And this is Tring.'

The boy pointed to the computer who, in response, turned a friendly sunshine yellow. 'An ancient meteorology AI I'm afraid, remade into a NannyBot for Laurie,' the computer added, proudly, with a little bow.

'This is our Sphereship, the *HoverSport* – we're anchored on the edge of the stratosphere, just beyond the Boxville mountains,' Laurie added.

Tring whirred to the opening, and pointed out the landscape beyond. 'This is the common room, out here we have the Clearing, beyond that we have the heaps – that's our store of junk to trade, all sorted into piles. Ferrous and non-ferrous metals, radioactives at the back, plastics and degradables just beyond the main paths—'

'That's it?' Atti interrupted, glancing at the huge opening to the massive junkyard on the deck of the ship. 'Where's the rest of the clan?'

The Junkers exchanged looks.

'We're all here,' Laurie said.

'But who's in charge?' Railey asked.

'I'm in charge.'

The computer coughed.

'And Tring too.'

'How did you get a whole Sphereship to yourself?' Railey said, still expecting some hideous Junker to appear from behind the heaps any minute. 'I thought Junkers were all about families, and hating all the other families and fighting for territory and ripping each other's arms off?'

Laurie's expression went dark.

'This is Laurie's family ship,' the computer said, looking at Laurie in a deep, sympathetic violet. 'Laurie and I are all that's left of this particular part of Clan Power .'

'What happened?'

The violet deepened. 'I don't think now is the time to delve into the family tree,' Tring said, with a nervous laugh.

The floor began to shudder.

Laurie looked up at the roof of the common room.

'Uh oh,' Care said, pulling her welding mask back down over her face.

Railey peered out at the Clearing.

The wind had dislodged junk from the heaps,

and bits of roller skate and microwave were blowing in twisty patterns in the air. There was a deepening hum of rotor blades slicing through the thin, cold atmosphere.

Tring motored back and forth in panic. 'Oh dear, oh dear, oh dear.'

Laurie pointed to Railey. 'You two need to hide. Now.'

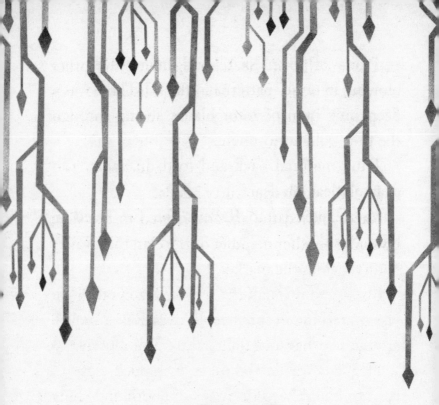

IZMAE

Railey ran up the slide and into the room with the blankets. She pulled one over her head and crept out on to the balcony, concealing herself behind the table. She peered over the edge and froze.

'It's him, Atti,' she whispered. 'The Junker from the market – Razor.'

The Junker with the pink mohawk was standing

in the middle of the Clearing with the other members of his clan. Highly polished metals hung from their necks and belts, and weapons of the sort Railey had seen for sale in the market – long crowbars, laser cutters, axes and hammers – were clutched in their dirty hands.

Razor sniffed the air, and moved to the side, revealing another member of the clan that Railey hadn't seen in the market.

She was tiny – half the size of Razor, but there was something in the sheepish way Razor moved around her that told Railey she was important.

Her hair was ice-white and cropped close to her head, and her skin was as smooth and shiny as new-formed aluminium. She would have been pretty, but for the way her head stuck out a little from her shoulders, which gave her the look of a hyena.

Railey knew in that instant that she did not want anything to do with this Junker.

Laurie emerged into the Clearing from the common room below in a flurry of dusty footsteps. Care and Tring followed, but stayed close to the doors.

'All right, Lau,' Razor smiled.

'Where's that smile, Lau?' another Junker added. Razor held out a hand and shushed them.

Laurie glanced weakly at Razor, but his eyes were set on the small Junker.

'It's not the normal business today, Lau,' Razor said, glancing back at the small woman. 'Just thought we'd drop in and say hello.' He waved a hand that was missing two fingers. 'So . . . hello.'

Atti caught a movement in the corner of his eye, the slightest twitch from the silver-haired Junker. A signal. A Junker with an eye patch and a nail gun nodded and quietly broke off from the group, disappearing into the shadows between the heaps.

'Where did he get this stuff?' the woman said suddenly. Everyone turned.

She picked up a torch from the heap beside her and threw it back down in disgust. 'There's better trade in a Boxville trader's toilet.' She sounded like she was going to be sick. 'This isn't a Sphereship – it's a bin. A great big bin in the sky.' She looked at Laurie. 'Your dad left you with a bin to live in. Are you happy about that?'

'Our main trade is charts, Izmae,' Laurie said. 'You know that. It's what our clan has always done. We're chart makers.'

'Izmae!' Atti hissed in Railey's ear. 'Chart makers! That's what Gran said—'

'Shush!' Railey clamped her hand over his snout.

'Bet you've forgotten what it feels like up there now, ay?' the woman continued, gesturing to the great blue sky above them. 'Up in the mesosphere with the other clans, where you belong, under the sparkling ceiling of the Soup. Feels better down here in the sun, does it?' She shook her head and looked at Laurie for a long time. 'Never seen anything so sad in my life,' she said softly.

Railey felt something strange pass between Izmae and Laurie in that moment. A shared sadness?

Razor laughed, bringing her attention away from Izmae. His expression reminded Railey of Welt and made her want to throw a big rock at him.

Laurie motioned to the common room. 'You want to see the charts?'

Izmae shook her head. 'No. No Junk Bomb business today, Laurie.'

Laurie was very still. The silence stretched out. 'Why the visit, then?' he said carefully.

Izmae was looking the heaps up and down again. The other Junkers were mirroring her movements, snarling at the stacks of office chairs and bicycles and shopping trolleys that dominated the piles around the Clearing.

'Well, it isn't to trade with you, that's for sure,' she said with a loud, booming laugh. Then stopped. 'Or maybe it is, a bit.'

Atti's head flicked to the back of the room.

Railey's heart leapt. 'What is it?'

He tugged her ear. 'Listen . . .'

Railey listened. Quiet footsteps rang on the staircase behind them.

'They're searching the Sphereship,' Atti whispered.

With no time to hide, Railey pulled the blanket over her feet and crouched tight against the balcony railing. The untidy room was full of piles of clothes and blankets. She hoped whoever was searching would think that she was just that.

Down in the Clearing, Izmae sidled up to Laurie and peered at him with her small hyena eyes.

'I'm not interested in your scribbles today,' she said. 'I'm looking for something more valuable.'

She paused, gauging Laurie's expression, then, peering right in Laurie's face, added, 'Apparently, the Pilot's been found.'

Laurie didn't move. Izmae rocked back on her heels.

'See, I've been sending my people down to Boxville for months, trying to figure out who this Pilot was. Whether it was even real, or just a nasty little rumour. And it could have been, for all we knew, because we couldn't find anyone, could we, Razor?'

'No, boss.'

'But turns out we weren't the only ones looking, were we Razor?'

'No, boss.'

'And because they weren't as thick as two steel panels, they figured it all out first.'

She was looking at Laurie, but her words were directed at Razor, who winced at every word.

'What Razor didn't realize was, it wasn't a some*one* we were looking for, it was a some*thing*, a machine – a little mechanical gecko to be precise, as yellow as the sun.'

Atti froze. Railey placed her hand on his back.

Behind them, the footsteps were louder, inside the room. Railey could hear the rustling of the chart papers, the furniture being shoved around. She scrunched up as small as she could under the blanket.

'Don't even breathe,' Atti whispered right in her ear.

Railey concentrated on Izmae's voice.

'Last thing Razor saw, before he let it get away.' Her voice drifted up to them. 'This gecko was running around the Junk Market with a girl – a horrible little Boxville dirt rat – and, worse than that, he said they were helped by a little Junker kid. Tiny thing, he said, big hair, big eyes, doesn't look well . . .' Izmae chewed her cheek and looked directly past Laurie at Care. 'You've got one of them, I think?'

Care pulled back behind Tring.

'Yeah, we've got someone who fits that

description,' Laurie said calmly, 'but then so do you.'

Izmae pulled up. 'What you talking about?'

Laurie pointed to a short Junker from Izmae's clan, who was inspecting a pair of roller skates. 'Small, big hair, big eyes,' he repeated, still pointing at the woman, who looked utterly confused. '. . . Doesn't look too well.'

Izmae turned around. 'Right. She's not nine though, she's fifty, and looks every year of it – no offence, Shaz. She's not getting mistaken for a kid at any speed. Plus, she wasn't in the Junk Market yesterday. I don't send her to the market because I don't trust her not to nick anything— Put that BACK, Shareen. We're Junkers, not thieves.'

Shaz took the roller skate out of her bag and stepped away from the heap.

Railey heard the boots leave the balcony and stomp back through the room and down the stairs.

She let out a long breath.

'Whoever it was with that Boxville girl, it wasn't one of us,' Laurie said coolly.

Izmae shook her head. 'Just like your dad,' she said, looking him dead in the eyes. 'He had dirt in his blood. Couldn't never trust him, should have known he'd betray us.' She narrowed her eyes. 'And now I'm wondering, are you betraying us too?'

'We weren't at the Junk Market. We hardly leave the ship, Iz, you know that.'

Izmae looked at him for a long time.

The Junker with the eye patch reappeared in the Clearing, and whispered something in her ear.

She clapped her hands together. 'OK, well, you do draw very well, very accurately, and you've been a great help in these challenging times. So, while we're in business, I'm not going to get in your way.'

Laurie visibly relaxed. Izmae stepped forward so she was face to face with him.

'In four days' time our business will be over, though, won't it?' she said with a smile. 'What are we going to do with you then?'

She called to the others and they trailed her back to the hovering gyros. As they mounted their machines, Izmae turned back.

'I'm calling a council,' she said. 'Your sad little clan will need to be represented.' She kicked the engine into gear. 'You know what to look for.'

With a burst of fans and dust and noise, Izmae and her clan had disappeared into the deep blue above.

As soon as they were out of sight, Laurie collapsed on to the ground. Care and Tring ran towards him and picked him up.

Railey ran down the slide as fast as her MagBoots would carry her. Atti was dancing from one shoulder to the other, his eyes wide and wild.

Railey stood blocking the doorway as the Junkers came up the ramp towards the common room.

'We're not moving until you tell us what's going on,' she said breathlessly.

Laurie looked defeated. 'OK.'

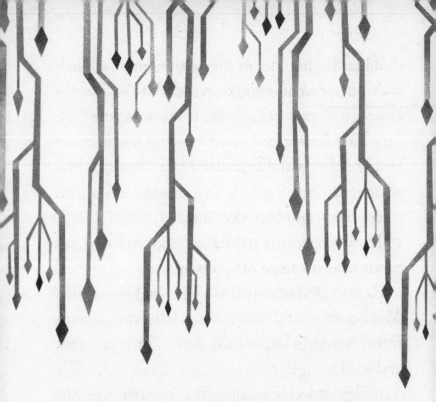

THE SCOPE ROOM

Laurie led them up the staircase, past the room with the blankets and up again, into a small, round room with a domed roof made out of hundreds of diamond-shaped glass panels. The sun was catching the angles of the panes, painting the room in a shimmering light; it was like stepping inside a gemstone.

She followed the Junkers inside and they stood

shoulder to shoulder in the hot, cramped space.

A huge machine took up most of the room – a single metal chair, tilted towards the sky, surrounded by complicated old cogs and mechanisms. A long tube extended from the top of the chair and out of a hole in the glass ceiling to where the bright blue sky shone.

'It's a scope, isn't it?' Railey said, running her hands over the huge old contraption.

Laurie nodded. 'My dad's. He used it to watch the Soup.'

'It's beautiful.' Railey sat down in the seat and looked through the telescope's eyepiece. She cranked the levers and pulleys on each side, but all she got was a disc of blinding sun.

'It works better at night,' Laurie said with a smile.

'What's all this?'

They turned in the direction of Atti's voice.

The diamonds of sunlight were cast over a series of charts stuck to the curved walls – more of the delicately drawn maps that Railey had seen when she'd first woken up on the Sphereship. But these were working charts – the intricate shapes drawn over in different colours, connected with thick red lines and covered in hastily scribbled notes.

'It's the Soup,' Railey said, moving closer. 'A map of all the objects in it.'

'It's some of them,' Laurie corrected her. 'The Soup's made up of billions of bits of junk – this is just the section Dad was working on.'

Railey peered at the charts. There were hundreds of shapes picked out in great detail. Railey recognized some – boxy satellites and massive cylindrical rocket boosters; smaller blocks that could be washing machines or dish-washers. There were cars and old train carriages, the fans from huge ventilation systems like the ones in the Junk Market, fuselages from planes and funnels from ships. Laurie and his dad had painstakingly mapped their position and projected orbit as they travelled around the Earth.

'I never knew there was so much up there,' Railey said, running her fingers along the lines of the drawings.

Tring sighed. 'Even the sky isn't big enough

for all mankind's waste.'

'From the meso it looks like stars,' Care said, staring at the hole in the domed roof dreamily. 'Lots of little tiny exploding stars.'

Railey tried to imagine the billions of bits of old cars and fridges and armchairs and the rest, zooming above their heads faster than bullets. Then she pictured Izmae and the other Junkers floating on their Sphereships in the mesosphere below it, and a dark feeling crept into her stomach.

Atti was leaning over her shoulder so far in the other direction that if he didn't have hold of Railey's hair he'd fall. He'd spotted something odd on the opposite wall.

'What's that?' he said.

Railey followed his gaze. In the centre of the wall, four giant pieces of chart paper had been taped together. A great shape was scribbled across them, the details drawn and redrawn a hundred times in a hundred different coloured inks.

'It's junk, just like the rest,' Laurie said with a sigh. 'Only this has been mashed together—'

'It's a Junk Bomb,' Care said.

Atti stared at the chart. 'Junk Bomb?'

Laurie frowned. 'The junk in the Soup spins around Earth at twenty-seven thousand kilometres per hour. There's too much up there, so bits of junk crash into each other all the time, and when they do, the heat and speed make the pieces fuse together.'

'It's called Kessler syndrome – the bigger the junk gets, the easier it is for it to get hit by other stuff. So the more junk hits, the bigger the fused chunk gets, until—'

'It falls out of orbit.' Railey stared at the drawing on the chart. She thought of the Cascade – something as tiny as a microwave careering out of orbit could destroy a whole containerblock when it hit – so this . . . She couldn't even think about the destruction it would cause.

'But you can scrap it, can't you? The Junkers can scrap it, like they do everything else?'

Care snorted.

'This wasn't created by chance,' Tring said.

'Izmae mentioned a Junk Bomb,' Atti said, turning to Laurie.

The boy took a deep breath. 'Izmae's clan created the Junk Bomb a long time ago. She's been using Dad's charts to track it ever since, and predict when it'll fall out of the Soup and hit.'

Atti stopped pacing. 'Hit? Hit what?'

Care shrugged. 'Glass City, obviously.'

Atti sat down on Railey's shoulder. 'But it'll—'

'Kill everyone in the city? Definitely. In Boxville? Probably. The shockwave might even destroy the Sphereships, but I don't think she's thought about that . . .' Laurie's voice trailed off. 'I don't think she's thought about a lot of things.'

There was something about the way he spoke about Izmae that felt strange. But Railey's mind was racing too fast to dwell on it for too long.

'When will it hit?' Railey almost didn't dare to ask.

'Izmae said in four days' time she'd have no use for you any more,' Atti said slowly.

Laurie nodded. 'It'll hit in four days, according to Dad's charts—'

'That's why we thought you knew the plan already,' Care said.

Railey looked at Laurie. 'But why?'

Laurie shrugged. 'Power. Territory. Hate. I don't know exactly.'

'But, to kill *everyone*?'

'The mesosphere does things to you,' Laurie said, his eyes somewhere else. 'It's easy to forget what makes us human.'

'The clans have been talking recently,' Tring said. 'Something has brought them together. United them. That hasn't happened in my lifetime.'

'And that is a *loooong* time.'

'Thank you, Care.'

'She's mad,' Railey said, thinking of Izmae's small, bright eyes.

Laurie nodded. 'She definitely is, yeah.'

Atti crossed his arms. 'And you're *helping* her?'

Laurie looked like he'd been struck. 'We're not *helping* her. Why do you think we rescued you?'

'*Kidnapped* them.'

'Not helping, Care.'

'It don't make sense,' Railey said. 'Why would you risk so much to rescue us? Why did you hide us from Izmae? Why me and Atti?'

Laurie took a long while to answer, like he was wrestling with his words.

'There've been rumours in the mesosphere for years, that some trader from Boxville found out about the Junk Bomb, and did something to stop it. Made something – a pilot that can fly into the Soup.'

Atti scoffed. 'No one can fly into the Soup. It's impenetrable. They'd get ripped to bits. No one has been into space since the last century. I'm a p—' He paused. 'I'm a pilot,' he said slowly, 'I should know.'

'You're right,' Laurie said, meeting Atti's eyes steadily. 'But if they're small enough, and nimble enough, with super hearing and eyes with 360-degree vision like a hawk –' he slowed his speech, and continued – 'if they were *designed* to do it, and if they've been training for it every day of their lives since they were made, then maybe, just maybe such a pilot could fly the Soup.'

Blood began to rush in Railey's ears.

Atti looked at her, his eyes searching hers.

'You're it, Atti,' she whispered. 'Gran made you for this. It makes sense of everything. She wasn't losing her mind at all.'

Atti stared back at the people staring at him. 'What?'

'Think about it – the races, the drones, the dodging the hoops and spinning though the figure of eight,' Railey said, slowly, watching Atti's face. 'The moving obstacles – she made us train *every day*, Atti. More than any others—'

Atti was incredulous. 'Because we had *terrible* parts. Because our drone wasn't good enough, we needed to fly it better—'

'No, Atti. It was because *you* needed to be better than a drone pilot. You needed to predict obstacles before you could even see them, fight the G-force in the corners—'

'You've had too much pop, Railey. The sugar's gone to your head.'

'You're the Pilot,' Tring said. 'We knew it as soon as we saw you at the race yesterday.'

Atti looked at his reflection in the domed windows. It was like he was seeing himself for the first time. He was designed for a purpose? How could this all be about him?

'But . . . I don't know how to fly the Soup, I

don't know how to stop a Junk Bomb.'

Laurie turned to the scope. 'I think that was Dad's part of the plan,' he said, inspecting the cogs and pulleys. 'But he's not here any more, so we need to think.'

'Just us?' Railey said. 'There's got to be someone else who can help us? An adult, at least?'

Care stuck out her bottom lip. 'Erm, Tring's two hundred years old, actually.'

Railey ignored her. 'What about the other Junkers? Surely another clan can help?'

Laurie shook his head. 'Every Junker in the Spheres hates Glass City for what they did to them. They might think she's crazy too, but they're with Izmae.'

'It's really just us?'

Laurie nodded.

The room went quiet. Atti felt pressed to the ground, like the gravity in the room had suddenly become stronger. How could it be him? How could Gran have planned all this without a single word? Was he really just a tool? A component in their plan?

Suddenly, he was angry too. He hadn't asked

for this. He hadn't asked to be made.

'There's been a mistake,' he said. 'This is all wrong.'

'Atti—' Railey's warm hand was on his back.

He shrugged her away. 'I need some air.' He jumped out through the hole in the roof and disappeared into the heaps.

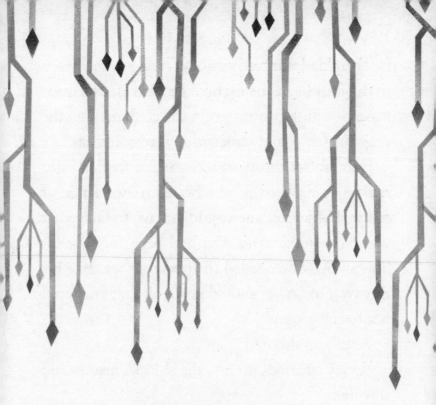

THE HEAPS

Railey crept as quietly as she could over the silvery solar cell path.

Night on the heaps had brought a darkness unlike anything she'd known in neon-lit Boxville. It wrapped the heaps in deep black shadows that seemed to lurch towards her with the snap of coats and the fizz of a broken robotic arm.

'Atti?' she called, as loud as she dared.

Tring had warned her about being in the heaps in the middle of the night. The metal in the great towers of junk contracted in the cold, making the piles unstable, and junk slides were common.

Junk slides didn't sound so bad to her right now – at least if she was buried under a pile of rusty old bicycles she wouldn't have to face what was happening. And Atti had been missing for hours now. She needed the gecko. It was like his tiny weight on her shoulder was all that anchored her to the ground.

'Atti!' she shouted again.

Railey peered up at the black heaps and shivered.

Everything on the ship felt wrong – bright daylight, the cold, the constant, quiet rumble of the engines. They'd only been on board for hours, and already Railey pined for the hot, dusty alleys of Boxville like she'd been away for years.

'ATTI!' she shouted again, kicking a desk lamp down the path. The clatter it made on the solar cells was a welcome distraction from the empty silence.

She'd spent the afternoon milling around the

common room waiting for Atti to return and staying out of the way.

She couldn't stand the way the Junkers looked at her – the disappointed glances that they didn't think she'd notice, the nervous whispers when they thought she couldn't hear.

Worst thing was, she didn't blame them. She was useless, wasn't she? If Gran had designed Atti for the Soup then what was Railey's role in this? Was she only needed as a cover to get Atti into the drone races? A shoulder for him to sit on? Was that all Gran thought of her?

She wrapped her arms around herself, but still the cold wind got through the gaps in her jacket and bit her skin.

'Atti!'

Nothing.

Railey sank down to the ground. She pulled her knees up to her chin and wrapped her skinny arms around them. Out of habit more than anything, she pulled Gran's goggles down and watched the diagnostics skim in front of her eyes, trying to focus on anything other than the deep, black hole that had opened up in her chest.

Then, the goggles picked up a light.

It was orange tungsten, way off in the distance, flickering like a candle as it moved between the heaps.

'Atti?' she whispered, but unless the gecko had grown three times his size in the last three hours, he couldn't hold a light that big.

Railey pushed herself back against the heap and watched the light pass by.

Her body tingled with curiosity. The type of curiosity that had got her into more trouble than she'd like, but it was a feeling she couldn't ignore. And it was better than being scared.

Tring had said that no one was allowed into the heaps after dark. So whoever it was out there was up to something – something secret – and Railey had too much of Boxville in her blood not to want to find out what it was.

Slowly, she got to her feet and crept towards the light.

It had come to rest on the edge of something low and smooth. There was the sound of rushing water, and suddenly the whole world was lit bright swimming-pool blue.

Railey jumped. The wash of light revealed that she was standing in the middle of another large clearing in the heaps, like the one outside the common room, but at the centre there was a raised pool, glowing with pale blue light.

Laurie was stood silhouetted against it.

'The heaps are off limits at night,' he said, without turning. He threw a bag of plastic pen lids into the pool and Railey heard the sound of bubbling liquid.

She walked over and peered into the pool. The surging liquid looked thicker than water.

'What is that?'

'Plaskton,' Laurie said, tipping another bag into the pool, this one containing colourful key rings. This time the water surged so high it nearly escaped over the edge.

'Careful,' Laurie said. 'They'll eat anything made out of plastic.' He pointed to Railey's goggles. She pulled them off her face and stashed them safely inside her jacket.

Without the tint of the goggles, she could see colours swirling in the blue water – pale green, apricot and lavender – iridescent, like the inside of a shell.

'It's beautiful. What does it do?'

Laurie sat down on the edge of the pool. 'Genetically modified plankton. They eat plastic, and produce oxygen.'

Railey nodded. 'Can I have a go?'

Laurie pointed to the heaps around the pool. They were stacked with different sun-bleached plastic junk – kids' toys, canoes, buckets, Tupper-ware, prams. Railey selected a hairdryer from the nearest heap and threw it into the pool. The water jumped up to meet it, frothing in anticipation.

'This is fun,' she said, launching another.

'The oxygen they make keeps the artificial atmosphere on the Sphereship working. Keeps us humans warm and breathing this high up in the Stratosphere.'

'That's clever.' Railey lugged an old car dash-board into the pool and watched the plaskton devour it greedily.

'In Boxville we got SteelSheep that hoover up all the scraps the market leaves behind – but I never seen anything like this.' She threw in a handful of toothbrushes and watched the water bubble. 'We could do with some more oxygen down there though – especially in the summer. We have air vents, but they don't do much. Too many containerblocks and too many sweaty bodies.'

She thought of Boxville and Gran and felt the hole in her chest open out.

'Dad loved Boxville,' Laurie said, smiling. 'We didn't trade much, but he still went down to the Junk Market every month. I always thought it was strange, but it makes sense now. He must've been meeting your Gran. Cooking up their plan.'

Railey nodded. 'Gran always said she was half Junker – no one ever believed her, not properly anyway. Now I think she said a lot of things that I thought weren't true that might be. She used to go missing a lot, before she had Atti and me to look after. She said she was in Glass City, trading, but I reckon she was meeting your dad.' She sighed. 'I spent every day with her, but I feel like I'm just getting to know her now – she never told me anything.'

Laurie sighed too. 'My dad didn't tell me either. I think they were just trying to keep us safe.'

Railey huffed. 'Didn't work, did it?'

She could see the tears in Laurie's eyes, but she didn't say anything. Laurie didn't seem like the kind of boy who wanted to talk about dead dads and grans – Railey was fine with that. He seemed nice enough, but he was still a Junker – and that meant she wasn't going to trust him in a hurry. But her curiosity kept nagging at her.

'What happened to your dad?' she said, unable to hold it in.

Laurie wiped his eyes. 'He fell off a heap.'

Railey looked around. 'One of these?'

Laurie smiled sadly. 'No. That's just what we say when a Junker dies. Doesn't matter when or where or how, they always just "fell off a heap".'

'Oh.'

Laurie nodded. There was obviously more to the story, but the expression on his face was suddenly so raw and angry she was too scared to ask.

'One minute he was there, the next he wasn't,' she said.

Laurie nodded.

Railey picked up a pair of melted sunglasses

and tossed them between her hands. 'Gran fell off a heap too, then,' she said, thinking of the look on Gran's face before she'd pushed her and Atti off the rooftop. 'I reckon she'd like the sound of that.'

Laurie smiled.

Railey threw a watering can into the liquid and watched it melt away. 'We always thought she was just mad, always going on about Junkers and the sky burning and stuff, but now I think she just kept getting the truth all jumbled up.'

'I found out through Dad's charts,' Laurie said. 'He'd designed it that way. It was like he knew what was going to happen to him. Dad was always better with charts than people. I think it was the only way he could have told me.'

'Least he told you something,' Railey said. 'Gran never told us anything other than we were drone racers. Don't know if she planned to tell us eventually or not, maybe before she lost her marbles . . .' She stopped. Something prickled in her consciousness, like an itch in the back of her mind. 'What did you just say? About the charts?'

Laurie frowned. 'Dad wasn't good at talking, he—'

'No, not that bit.'

'He left the Junk Bomb in his charts for me to find?'

Railey stood up. 'Yes,' she said. 'That's it.' She turned to Laurie. 'That's exactly it!'

The Junker stood up too, dislodging a pile of CDs from the side of the vat and sending them tumbling into the water.

Railey was grinning from ear to ear.

'Why go to all the trouble of making Atti and training him up all our lives but not give us a plan? It don't make sense.'

Laurie shook his head. 'No. It doesn't.'

'So that means there *must* be a plan, somewhere. We just have to find it.'

Laurie frowned.

Railey grabbed his arm and pulled him back through the dark heaps towards the common room.

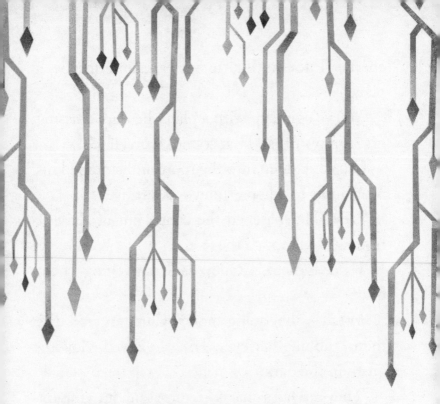

THE SECRET DRONE

Railey ran through the common room and launched herself up the red plastic stairs to the scope room. Panting, she pulled the charts from the walls and spread them out on the floor.

She didn't notice Atti until his toes were scratching the side of her neck.

'Where've you been?' he yawned.

'Looking for you,' she said, scanning the

charts. 'I found Laurie instead, and maybe a plan.'

'You've come up with a plan?' he said, crossing his stumpy arms. 'That sounds worrying.'

Laurie skidded into the room and stomped his MagBoots to where Railey was sitting.

'Hey!' He snatched the charts out of Railey's hands. 'Don't touch those.'

'I need them,' Railey said, snatching them back.

'What's she doing now?' Care entered the room, rubbing her eyes. Tring followed, glowing green in the dark.

'They're Dad's charts,' Laurie said, lunging for the papers again, but Railey pulled them back before he could reach them.

'And they'll be nothing but ashes like everything else if that Junk Bomb hits,' she said. 'Right?'

Laurie rocked back on his heels and sat down, defeated.

'Thought so.'

Railey pulled the charts back into the formation she'd been playing with. Her hands were sweaty and slippery, and she was leaving big greasy prints all over the delicate paper sheets, but she could already see that something was coming together.

'I thought these looked wonky when I saw them,' she explained. Laurie leant over her shoulder, covering it in silvery metal dust. Railey flicked her multitool to the torch attachment and passed it to him.

'Hold this. Look, these red lines here don't do nothing other than complicate things,' she said, running her fingers over the thick red lines that connected the junk in the Soup. 'If your dad was the best chart maker you Junkers got, then the last thing he'd do is make lines for no reason.'

She squinted at one page, and laid it out at an angle across the other.

'Ah! Look, see that?'

Atti jumped up on to Railey's head and peered at the charts. It took him a couple of seconds, but . . .

'Oh, yes. Look at that.'

The Junkers moved behind Railey, each peering at the spot where the orange beam of the torch was pointing.

'Why are you showing us a drawing of a bird?' Care appeared in Railey's armpit, chewing on a length of some processed sugary thing that smelt like lemons. 'It's not even *good*.'

Railey gritted her teeth. 'It's not a bird.'

'It's a plan,' Atti cut in, walking towards the centre of the sheets of paper and pointing to the place where the red lines overlapped, creating an uneven boxy shape with four circles spinning off it. 'This is the way we stop the Junk Bomb.'

'I don't think a bird is going to help.'

'It's not a bird, Care.'

'It's the Fox,' Railey said, sitting back and grinning. 'It's a blueprint for the Fox.'

'I don't think a fox is going to help either—'

'It's our racing drone – the Fox – but with different attachments.' Railey's eyes took the drawing in greedily – the original Fox had been retrofitted with a fuel-powered launch capsule, and collapsible rotor blades for the journey back into the thicker air of the stratosphere. There was a proper cockpit for Atti, too.

Railey cocked her head and tried to make

sense of the attachment on the front. Laurie leant over her shoulder.

'It's a debris harpoon,' he said.

'A what?'

'Junker's use them to spear junk in the meso and drag it back to their Sphereship to scrap. I guess this one is designed to drag the Junk Bomb the other way – away from the Earth.'

Railey grinned at Atti. 'Slingshot,' they said in unison.

The slingshot was their trap in the races. Gran had been training Atti to slingshot the other drones out of his way for years. Railey wondered how she could ever have thought Gran was mad.

She examined the plans. It was like Gran was right there with them, communicating with her through Laurie's dad's beautiful drawings. She'd taught Railey to understand schematics and blueprints. She'd made sure she would know how to build this. A warm feeling spread through her – this wasn't all about Atti, this plan needed Railey too.

She was already thinking of the junk she'd seen in the heaps and how she could remake those parts to fit the drawings. 'They planned it all out,' she whispered, running her fingers over the red lines. 'It's all in the heaps, I've seen it.'

She looked at Laurie. 'I can make this,' she said. 'I've built and rebuilt the Fox a million times, I can do this.'

'But can you do it in three days?' Laurie said, eyes following her hands. 'It still looks like a bunch of lines to me.'

Tring's screen lit the room icy blue. 'I can help,' he said. 'I understand engineering plans.'

Railey pushed her fringe out of her eyes. 'And we'll need Care to help us search for parts in the heaps.'

Atti licked his eyes. 'I'll need time to get used to the new controls.'

The Fox laid out in the hidden plans looked sleeker and faster and more powerful than the one Atti flew around the arena – if this was any other time he'd be itching to get inside the newly designed cockpit, but this wasn't like any of the other times.

He could feel Railey's eyes on him, silently checking he was OK and not planning to disappear again.

She was right to be worried. Atti's tiny stomach had been flip-flopping ever since he'd heard about the Junk Bomb and his role in defeating it. He'd always known he'd been made, but being made for a purpose – this purpose – was too much for even his advanced mind to compute. He wasn't sure if he was excited or terrified.

He looked up at the brightening sky, and tried to imagine swooping and ducking through the endless, spinning junk of the Soup. He couldn't. It all seemed utterly impossible.

Railey brushed her hand along his back, so slightly that the others wouldn't notice. Warmth pulsed through his body at her touch, and he felt a little steadier – just like the races, they were in this together.

Until the Soup, he thought. Railey could only be with him for so long. Inside the Soup he'd be completely alone.

Atti concentrated on supervising Railey as she scribbled a list of components on the wall. There was no time to waste. Laurie paced up and down, giving Care and Tring directions to which heaps might hold the parts they were listing, and the girl uh-huh-ed and nodded like she really was listening.

They spent the rest of the dark early morning searching the heaps for the parts scribbled on the wall, the Boxville girl, the gecko and the Junkers working together as seamlessly as if they'd known each other for years, not hours.

Soon, as the sun began to burn deep purple into the edges of the sky, they all gathered beside the pile of parts, exhausted, but with something like excitement simmering in the air between them.

Only Tring seemed distant. He roved up and down the room, his screen pointed up above their heads to the place in the dome where the brass scope pierced the glass and continued into the sky.

'Oh dear,' he muttered, turning the colour of a storm cloud. 'Oh no.'

The others looked up.

'What is it, Tring?' Laurie said.

The computer pointed his pincer arm at the

sky. Atti peered up and saw the blackness was painted with great swathes of bright red and green.

Care gasped.

'Oh, not now,' Laurie mumbled. 'It can't be. Not now.'

Tring looked him in the eye, his screen now the colour of blood. 'The aurora has her reasons, I'm sure,' he said, turning away. 'I'll get the ship ready.'

Railey and Atti exchanged a look.

'What's going on?' the gecko said. 'Who's Aurora?'

'Why's everyone so scared?'

Care rolled her eyes. 'It's Junkers' business,' she said, disappearing down the stairway after Laurie and Tring.

Railey looked at Atti and then launched herself down the stairs after them.

Junkers' business had a lot to do with them these days.

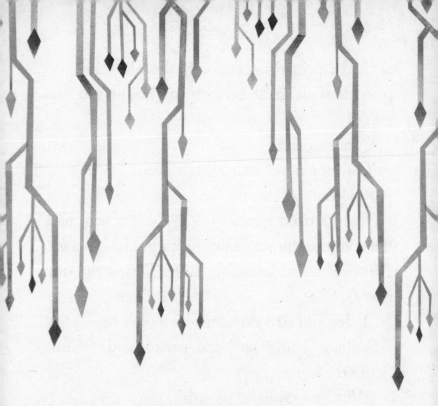

THE SOUP

The ground leapt under them, and Railey rolled down the last few steps of the staircase head over MagBooted heels.

Atti was standing in front of her face, smiling wickedly. 'I know it used to be a slide, Railey, but they remade the steps for a reason.'

She ignored him. 'They've powered up the engines?'

He nodded. 'We must be going somewhere.'

Railey scrambled to her feet. The ground was vibrating violently beneath her boots. Atti was right. Railey had forgotten the huge ship could actually move.

Atti jumped on to her collar and she ran out on to the balcony where the Junkers had gathered, staring silently at the trembling heaps.

Above them, great swathes of green and red light moved through the dark like silk curtains, swooping and swaying in some unseen breeze.

'What *is* that?' Atti asked.

'It's the aurora borealis,' Laurie said, glancing at him before pulling his attention back to the sky. He had a plastic tube strapped across his chest, with rolls of chart paper curling out of the end. 'It's the sun sending bursts of electro-magnetic energy towards Earth's spheres,' he continued, hugging the tube to his chest.

'Where are we going?' Railey asked, getting annoyed. She glanced at the computer beside her. 'And what's wrong with Tring?'

The computer's coloured screen had been replaced with white scrolling code. Railey knew code of course, but the letters and symbols were going so fast she couldn't make any of it out.

'He's launching the ship into the mesosphere,' Laurie said. 'Into the aurora.'

'But *why*?' Railey snapped, anger prickling at her skin. 'Where are we going?'

Laurie looked at the tube. 'It's a Junkers' Council,' he said. 'All the clan leaders must attend.' He tapped the charts piling out of the end. 'Even the chart makers.'

Tring shook his screen and flicked back to a deep navy blue.

'The first council in over fifty years, I believe,' he said, in a voice that sounded like he'd just woken up. 'Most inconvenient, but our lack of presence will cause more problems than us being there, so we must attend.'

'Izmae made this, too?' Atti said, staring at the colourful sky.

Care laughed. 'Er, no. She's not magic.'

Laurie yawned. 'Councils take place during the first appearance of the aurora after the council is called. They say it's for ceremonial purposes, but it has a lot more to do with the electromagnetism blocking their radio signals so Glass City can't snoop on them.'

'But why did they stop?'

'Because of all the fighting,' Care said, pulling a taser from her belt and letting a fork of electricity spit out of the probes. 'And all the murders.'

Tring flicked to a worried green. 'Well, yes, things did get a little out of hand at times, but the main aim of the council was to discuss territory, salvage rights—'

'And to kill other people's clans,' Care said, wickedly. 'Just *zap*, *zap*, *stab*, *zap*, *crush* —' she pulled the trigger on imaginary laser cutters and swung an imaginary wrench – 'all dead.'

Laurie's jaw tightened.

'This is Izmae's moment. Bringing us all together again, to celebrate the Junk Bomb and the end of Glass City.'

'But shouldn't we be concentrating on building the drone?' Railey said.

'That's what you'll be doing while we're at the council,' Laurie said. 'You'll stay inside the common room, and don't make any noise. No sparks either – they'll see those.'

'You're just going to leave us?'

'Look, Railey,' Atti whispered, tapping her cheek with his toes, 'stars.'

Railey lifted her head and her breath caught.

The ship had already left the earthly trappings of the stratosphere. Now, the curve of the Earth fell away from the ship on either side, and the black around them was wrapped in the smoky white halo of the outer atmosphere. A band of white and red pinpricks glittered in the deep blue curve of sky above them. Faint lights travelling fast across the curve, winking out from milky clouds of vapour and gas.

Railey's mouth fell open. She'd never seen the stars before – even the Cascade couldn't live up to this. There must be billions of them.

'They're not the stars,' Laurie sighed. 'That's a million-billion chunks of metal and plastic crashing into each other at over twenty-seven thousand kilometres per hour – otherwise known as the Soup.'

The Soup.

Railey stared at it in wonder. For an instant she forgot about Gran and the Sphereship and

Izmae's war and everything else. All she could think about was how beautiful it was.

She had always imagined the Soup to be an ugly thing, a dirty thing. But from here it looked like a shoal of tiny, bright fish swimming in a dark sea, darting and snaking and flickering their silver and gold scales in the moonlight.

'A hundred years of human rubbish,' Laurie said with a shake of his head.

'It's beautiful,' Atti said.

Railey smiled. 'I never thought in all my life that I'd actually see the Soup with my own eyes.'

Atti nodded back, then his attention was caught by something else. 'What's that?' he said, pointing to a cluster of black dots coming into view up ahead.

Railey pulled Gran's goggles down over her eyes.

The lenses zoomed in and she could just make out several bulky shapes emerging between the flowing curtains of green light.

'Are they Sphereships?'

Then, as if she'd just commanded it, the objects burst into colour with a thousand blinking tungsten lights.

'The signal.' Laurie glanced at Tring.

The computer's screen began to flicker with code again, and one by one the lights on the *HoverSport*'s deck buzzed back to life.

'Show's about to start,' Laurie muttered, adjusting the chart tube nervously.

Railey's eyes were fixed on the glowing armada of remade ships that were lighting up the sky around them, for as far as her goggles would reach.

Her heart began to thud against her ribs.

This wasn't her world any more.

It wasn't even Laurie's.

The bright, sunny world of the stratosphere seemed a million miles away from this – the real world of the Junkers, dark and deadly.

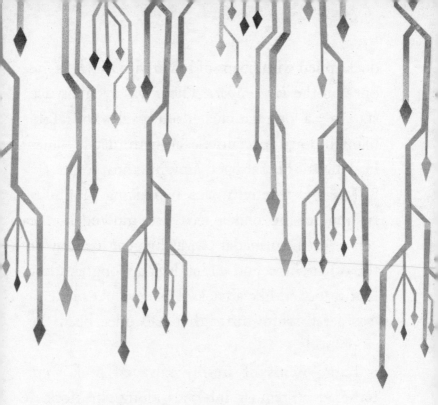

THE KNOCK

As the *HoverSport* cruised steadily towards them, Railey began to pick out more detail in the Sphereships hovering silently under the sparkling ceiling of the Soup.

Each was remade from an Earth vessel – there were huge cruise ships with their cabins and decks ripped out and replaced with piles of twisted metal, military aircraft carriers, their decks piled with heaps of junk twice as tall as the ones on the *HoverSport*. There was even a space station – a long flat cluster of capsules with 'ISS' painted down its centre, each with rusted cranes heaving freshly salvaged junk into heaps.

The most activity was happening around a rusting red oil tanker that was moored in the centre of the armada. It was bigger than any of the other ships, and had a deck so long and low that it looked like a trick of the eye. At one end was a tall white turret that had once been the ship's bridge.

Large items of freshly salvaged junk were tethered at regular intervals along the deck – aeroplanes, satellites, rocket boosters, double-decker buses – all spitting with the brightly coloured sparks of laser cutters wielded by unseen Junkers as they tore them apart.

Railey felt the *HoverSport*'s engines slow, and Tring rejoined them on the balcony.

'That is Izmaes's Sphereship,' he explained. 'It's called the *Knock* – a remade oil tanker, from the days when Earth ran on fossil fuels.'

Railey nodded.

Tring shook his screen. 'I have a very bad feeling about this, Laurie,' he said, flicking through the colours of storm clouds.

'You have a bad feeling about everything,' Laurie replied, looking forward as the ships grew closer.

'Izmae will see this as an opportunity,' the computer said. 'If they already suspect we have the Pilot . . . We're outnumbered, outmanned, out-weaponed . . .'

'You think this is a trap?' Atti said.

'I hope so,' Care growled, her taser spitting in the dark. Railey jumped away from the sparks.

Laurie shook his head. 'Izmae could have attacked us with the crew she brought to see us yesterday.' He frowned. 'I think she's watching us, waiting for us to make the first move.'

'We're using war tactics now, then. How depressing.'

'This is a war.' Laurie's teeth were gritted. 'You two better get out of sight. You too, Care.'

The girl made a face but did as she was told and moved inside.

Tring piloted the Sphereship through the

smaller vessels moving between the armada ships, and pulled up silently alongside the great red edge of the tanker.

The ship's name was written in letters as high as a container along its side – with a tiny metal staircase winding up through the K and N like a black vein.

Laurie pulled a helmet over his rusty hair.

'Stay hidden,' he said, hoisting himself and his chart tube on to the rickety stairs. His MagBoots flickered green as they attracted to the steps. Tring followed.

'Be safe,' the computer whispered, before whirring up the stairs behind Laurie.

'What do we do now, then?' Railey said a few minutes later, turning to Care, who had collapsed into the Chesterfield, and was carving something into the arm with a knife.

'Er, sleep? Or make a drone? Eat some floss. Play arcade – I don't know, I'm not your mum.'

Railey yawned. 'Helpful, Care, thanks.'

She should be exhausted – she hadn't slept since she'd woken up on the Sphereship the day before, and they'd been up all night scouring the heaps for parts for the secret drone – but there was too much adrenaline in her veins, too many plans forming in her head. The last thing she wanted to do was rest.

Atti obviously felt the same. He paced the common room anxiously, scurrying along the edges of the windows, trying to get a look at the deck of the *Knock* without being seen – but they were docked too low and all he could see was the never-ending hull and the salvaged airliner that was being dismantled high above their heads.

'What do you think's happening up there?' There was a shake in his voice.

Care settled futher into the chair. 'More fun things than down here. Lau's taken his fighting wrench with him, so *something's* going to happen.' She sighed. 'Should have taken me, not Tring – I'm the best junk diver in the hemisphere—'

'What's a junk diver?' Atti asked.

The girl shook her head. 'You'll see.'

Railey huffed. She couldn't imagine the skinny nine-year-old being any help against an angry

Junker, taser or not.

If Care noticed Railey's frustration, she didn't show it. Instead she continued to sulk. 'But I'm here making sure you don't die or run away or anything.'

'Well, that's reassuring, thank you.'

'You're not welcome.' She pulled her welding mask down, signalling the end of the conversation.

Railey busied herself with the parts for the new drone, while Care lay in the Chesterfield, staring at the ceiling as she popped sweets under the welding mask and into her mouth. Atti still couldn't settle. A strange feeling had settled in his circuits. Like the sensation of being watched.

He moved across the common room ceiling, crawled through the ventilation panel on the back wall and along the air duct, before poking his head out the vent at the other end. There was a line of small, narrow heaps, and then the sheer red hull of the *Knock*. Not daring to ignore Laurie's order and go outside, instead he tilted his head until he could make out the thin black line of the ship's staircase.

All the time the strange sensation burnt his

circuits. He couldn't see anything wrong, but the feeling was making him twitchy.

He was about to turn back to the common room when he heard the faintest shuffle of boots.

In the same second, Razor appeared from between the heaps, a huge laser cutter humming in his hand. He sniffed the air, like a dog with a scent, then padded carefully towards Atti's hiding place.

Atti froze. He guessed the shadow inside the vent must be concealing him, but Razor was so close he could touch him.

The Junker looked left and right. Then disappeared around the corner.

Panting, Atti backed along the duct, ran across the ceiling and launched himself at Railey.

'He's here!' he hissed, clutching her earlobe and pulling hard.

'Ow! What?'

'Razor!' he squeaked. 'On the ship!'

Care jumped up. 'Where?'

'In the heaps –' he pointed to the vent – 'he's coming around this way.'

The scuff of MagBoots on metal made them

all turn towards the opening to the Clearing.

Care pulled Railey to the floor and peeped over the Chesterfield.

Three more Junkers appeared from between the heaps around the Clearing, creeping as best as they could in their clinking metal armour.

'They're everywhere,' Railey said. 'We're trapped.'

Atti pulled on her ear again. 'This way.'

He jumped off her shoulder and scurried back along the common room wall towards the vent, nodding for the girls to follow.

He pushed the cover up with his snout and beckoned for them to crawl through into the duct. Railey was skinny enough, and Care was nothing but a string of spaghetti in comparison. They'd fit.

Railey hesitated. 'But where are we going to go if the heaps are full of Junkers?'

'Up there.' Atti pointed to the staircase that led to the deck of the *Knock*.

Railey crossed her arms. 'So we're escaping this ship, on to that ship, where there are even *more* Junkers? That makes sense.'

'I like it,' Care said, giving Railey a look as she pushed her aside and followed Atti into the duct.

Railey glanced in the direction of the scope room. 'But the drone parts are spread all over the floor – they'll see them!'

Care turned back. 'Junkers pull things apart. They don't understand putting things together – all Razor will see is parts, trust me.'

Railey watched them go. 'We're *really* doing this?'

She could hear Razor now, whispering too loudly to the others as they surrounded the common room.

Atti's head reappeared at the panel. 'If you've got any other ideas I'd love to hear them, Railey,' he hissed.

Railey couldn't think of anything. If they stayed on the *HoverSport*, the Junkers would find them eventually. The *Knock* would be the last place they'd look for them.

'C'mon,' the gecko said, 'and try not to be clumsy and loud.'

Railey pulled Gran's goggles down around her neck and put the helmet with the cracked visor on. With a last glance back to the common room, she wriggled through the vent.

'*I'm* clumsy?' she whispered, right in Atti's ear. 'Don't you remember the time you knocked Gran's glass jar over into her synth burger? The only bit of real glass we ever owned!' She pulled herself out the other side of the duct and landed softly in the dust.

'And that time in the market,' she continued, stepping carefully between the heaps, 'when you dropped your dinner into Krys's lap just as I was about to seal the deal on those edibles?'

Atti scampered up on to the handrail of the staircase. 'How was I supposed to know he was scared of grasshoppers?'

'I don't think he was *scared*, Atti. It's just half munched-up hoppers are disgusting to everyone but you.'

Care pushed Railey up the stairs with the end of her taser. 'Ugh, please stop fighting and go!'

They crept up the stairs, away from one danger, headed straight into another, much bigger one.

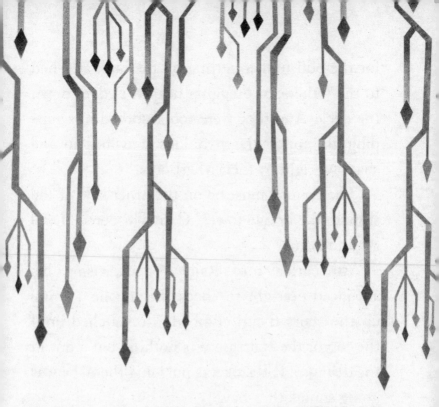

THE JUNKERS' COUNCIL

The deck of the *Knock* was an endless maze of thick red pipes and low, fat heaps.

'This way,' Care whispered, disappearing under a cluster of huge pipes that ran the length of the deck, and were held on struts high enough to crawl under. Hidden in the shadows, they made their way to the other side of the ship.

This part of the Sphereship was deserted, save

for the odd Junker cutting up the junk attached to the tethers, or dragging heaped sledges down the deck. And they were too absorbed in scrapping to notice the two kids crawling in the shadows right by their MagBoots.

'The council must be on the other side of the ship, in the bridge tower,' Care whispered. 'Let's go find Lau.'

Atti curled into Railey's neck, using his advanced eyesight to check for anyone coming up the stairs they'd climbed. He watched until the top of the staircase was nothing but a dot in the distance. If Razor was pursuing them, he was going some other way.

The deck of the *Knock* was so long that when Care finally put up a hand to slow them, Railey's legs were wobbly.

She sat down to catch her breath. Hidden beneath the pipes, Railey hadn't noticed the growing number of filthy MagBoots gathering either side of them. When Care stopped her, and she finally looked up, she realized that they'd run into the centre of a dense crowd of Junkers.

The white turret that Railey had seen from the

Sphereship now towered in front of them. Around its base, hundreds of Junkers were gathered, heads upturned, listening avidly to the person speaking to them through a sound system remade from the pipes of an ornate church organ.

Care sat down and pulled off her mask.

'It's OK,' she said. 'They have plaskton here too, so you can breathe on the deck.'

Railey pulled the cracked visor of her helmet up.

She could hear Atti breathing heavily in her ear, his tiny toes pressing deep into her neck. She held her hand beside him and felt him squeeze it.

'This was a bad idea,' he whispered. 'This was the worst idea you've ever had.'

'*My* idea? It was *your* idea!'

'Shhhh!'

Care pointed to a gap in the pipe above them. Railey readjusted her bum and the top of the turret came into full view.

Izmae was standing in the centre of a semi-circle of other Junkers, each twice as tall and twice as fierce-looking as her.

'They're the clan leaders,' Care whispered.

Each clan leader wore adornments that spoke of their junking heritage, in the same way that Laurie wore his chart tube around him like a sash. One tall, skinny Junker was decorated with rainbows of brightly coloured, sun-bleached plastics; another was covered head to toe in an armour made from the black shards of broken tablet screens; the biggest of the bunch, the one currently speaking, was wearing an intricate robe made of braided wires. His hair was braided too, and hung down to his waist.

Beside these behemoths, small, rusty, unadorned Laurie looked a bit silly.

'. . . The line has been drawn on charts since our families were banished into the Spheres. I don't understand the Plastic Islanders' reason for disputing—' the big Junker with the braids was saying.

'It's ours by right,' the multi-coloured Junker cut in, stepping forward. 'It was our junk that made the Plastic Isles, it's our right that we scrap the Soup above it—'

'Typical of Jockovic,' the Junker with the

screen armour sneered. 'Thinking everything you touch is yours.'

'Ha! That really is something coming from a D'Souza. How are the Santés these days?'

'I heard they were all dead,' another Junker interjected.

Screen Armour sneered. 'Rumours.'

'I don't see any of them here.'

The crowds around Railey rumbled. She felt like she was in the barrel of a PunchGun, waiting for it to explode.

The clans were all pushed together, shoulder-to-shoulder, for the first time in half a century. Each one armed and each one angry at the territory grabs and fighting that had happened between this council and the last. Izmae, a white-gold speck between the other leaders, stayed quiet as they argued to the crowds though the remade organ pipes.

In the midst of the clan leaders, Laurie kept his head down, and clutched his chart tube to his chest.

'There's going to be trouble,' Care said, her big eyes darting around the crowd, her fingers caressing her taser. 'I can feel it. Big trouble.'

'Why are they arguing about territory when they're planning to destroy half the cities in the hemisphere in three days?'

'Junkers *loooove* territory,' the girl said. 'They love territory more than air.'

A dull smacking sound echoed through the organ pipes. Railey looked up. Screen Armour had punched the Junker from above the Plastic Isles and the top of the turret was now a flailing mess of arms and weaponry.

There was a scuffle somewhere in the crowd near them. Care tensed up, ready to pounce, but the fight didn't have time to travel close enough to them before a loud voice interrupted.

'ENOUGH!'

The fighting instantly stopped. Railey spotted Laurie pawing at his mouth, mopping up blood.

'Animals,' Izmae snapped, stepping forward. She was wearing MagBoots with big platformed soles today, but still the others towered over her. 'Why do we always have to behave like animals?'

The other Junkers stood up straight, but with jaws jutted and their eyes bouncing around, watching the others.

'Animals don't think about the future. Maybe that's why we've got ourselves into this mess.'

The crowd started to rumble again.

'You lot can shut up!' Izmae shouted down an organ pipe, so her voice reverberated around the deck. 'If you've got an opinion – which I recommend you don't because I guarantee it will be stupid – tell your clan leaders –' she gestured to the men in the arc around her – 'and they will pass it on to me, the leader of the council, if they deem it fit. That's how a council works. OK?

'Territory –' she continued, only to be drowned out by the jeers of the crowd – 'TERRITORY!' she shouted, then pulled back, and shot a blast from her laser cutter into the crowd.

Railey heard a yelp from somewhere near the front and the thud of something heavy and soft falling to the deck.

The anger in the crowd went down to a simmer, but it didn't go away.

'They don't like her?' Railey asked Care.

'The other clans don't . . . and she just lasered someone's arm off. Now shush.'

Railey bristled. She was getting so sick of Care treating her like she was a kid. *Care* was the kid.

'Territory,' Izmae continued slowly, 'will be no use to us when there is no Soup left to scrap.'

The crowd settled a little.

'Glass City want to get rid of the Soup. They want to use their big laser to blast all the junk away so the people down there in their big glass towers can be safe from the Cascade.'

More jeers erupted around them, but this time aimed at Glass City.

Railey and Atti shared a glance. Could Glass City really do that? Did they have the power to destroy something as big and out of control as the Soup? Izmae and the Junkers clearly thought so.

'No Soup means no trade. No trade means no power. And no power means . . . no more Junkers.'

The stomping of the crowd's MagBoots was making the deck bounce beneath them.

Izmae was up on the thin edge of the platform, gesturing wildly with her laser cutter still in her grip.

'Clans don't matter!' she shouted. 'Feuds don't

matter. Because if we don't stop acting like animals and think about the future, before you know it Glass City will point their laser right up yer bum and turn you into a cloud of carbon dandruff. PUFF!'

Laughter rippled around them. Even Care guffawed into her gloves. Railey looked at her.

'What? She's funny.'

Izmae waited for the laughter to die down, grinning at the clan leaders. She walked to where Laurie was prodding his fat lip with his finger.

She pulled him to the edge by his chart tube. His eyes bulged.

'Look at me, you stupid dirt lover,' she growled, then whispered so it was only just audible down the pipes. 'Are we ready then, chart maker?'

Laurie gave a tiny nod.

There it was again, that strange familiarity between them. Railey frowned.

Izmae turned away from Laurie back to the crowd.

'But Junkers won't be bullied,' she shouted, parading back and forth. 'So we'll destroy them just like they want to destroy us!'

The crowd rumbled.

She turned her head up to the Soup, glittering high above them, and spread her arms wide, as if embracing the heavens.

'This,' she began, a smile spreading across her perfect face, 'is how we're going to destroy them.'

Railey turned her neck to see what Izmae was looking at. As she did, she saw the silvery shoals of rubbish in the Soup jump and bulge and scatter.

The Junkers in the crowd gasped.

Railey caught the edge of something moving deep inside the Soup, making the other items of junk and debris spinning in its vortex look as small as pieces of confetti. She couldn't make out its shape, or any detail at all, but she felt its colossal presence above them, like the air had grown heavier as it passed by, and the atmosphere was struggling under its weight.

'Pretty, isn't it,' Izmae beamed.

Laurie was staring at the floor. So *that* was the Junk Bomb business Izmae had mentioned yesterday in the Clearing – Laurie had charted the Junk Bomb and told Izmae exactly when and where it would pass overhead on its orbit inside the Soup. He'd contributed to this spectacle she'd engineered. The spectacle that had stunned the hundreds of Junkers in the crowd to silence.

'Our Junk Bomb −' Izmae said, her voice faltering with emotion − 'bigger than we thought, going faster than we thought − so it will cause more destruction than we thought!'

The crowd suddenly cheered.

Izmae jumped up on to the edge of the roof, her MagBoots allowing her to hang off the metal at an impossible angle.

'Glass City want to destroy our Soup!' she cried.

'BOO HOO!' someone shouted, creating a roar of laughter.

'But Junkers don't die, Junkers thrive! They should have learnt their lesson after they exiled our families into the Spheres.' Izmae shouted into the organ pipes, 'They expected us to die, but no, we built our Sphereships and spread all over the world, we created trade with Boxville and the other recycled cities, even them rotten Plastic Isles that Jonti is so keen to get his greasy hands on.' Another jeer; the multi-coloured Junker sneered.

'In three days' time,' Izmae continued, 'our Junk Bomb will give them a Cascade like they've NEVER seen before!'

A roar.

'And then . . . THEN . . . we can talk about territory. Not JUST in the Spheres –' she paused for dramatic effect – 'but on the ground too.'

The roar was deafening now. Atti pushed his toes into his ears.

Izmae was having to shout above the crowds now.

'You can have the Plastic Isles, Jonti, mate. You can all have anything you want – fight it out among yourselves. Soon all the ground and sky will be run by Junkers. And Glass City will know what it feels like to live in the rust!'

Whilst the crowd was fixated on congratulating themselves, Malik, the Junker with the braided coat, was stepping forward.

'What about the Pilot?' he said, directly into the pipes so the crowd could hear.

Only the word 'pilot' made it through the

noise, but that was enough.

The deck of the *Knock* was silenced.

Izmae spun on her heels and eyed Malik. The big man stared back, unmoving. A brick wall.

'There is no Pilot. So there's nothing to worry about,' she said slowly.

Malik shook his head. 'There was a Runner in Boxville two days ago.'

Railey's heart leapt into her mouth. Did Izmae glance at Laurie?

'Word is he's found the Pilot, and they got away – out of the city – on the *loose*.'

Malik paused for long enough for the crowd to start murmuring.

'Junkers from your clan were chasing too, right through the Junk Market,' the big Junker continued, 'right in front of the boots of all the junk traders from all the clans—'

'You shouldn't listen to what you hear from the junk traders, Malik – bunch of professional liars.'

Under the pipe, Railey caught Atti's eye.

'Izmae didn't send Nox after us?' he asked.

Railey held his gaze. 'Then who did?'

'Shush,' Care said, prodding them with her taser.

Atti shushed, but his head was spinning. Who was Nox working for, if not the Junkers?

'If the Pilot is free,' Malik said, rounding on Izmae, 'then they're free to stop the Junk Bomb, and you will fail.'

Jeers erupted from below. Malik smiled at Izmae.

'The Junk Bomb can't be stopped,' Izmae growled, rounding on the big man. 'In three days' time, it'll fall down into the meso and on to Glass City—'

'Unless the Pilot gets there first.'

The crowd began to shout and jeer. Izmae pushed Malik away and gestured wildly at the crowds below. 'IT CAN'T BE STOPPED!' she screamed into the organ pipes. 'IT CAN'T BE STOPPED!'

Railey could hear the tell-tale thuds of a fist fight somewhere in the crowd by the base of the turret, followed by the buzz of laser cutters.

Care sniffed the air and popped her head out from under the pipe. When she pulled back in, her eyes were wild.

'Big fight!' she said. 'I told you there was always a fight! Bet it's Malik's clan and the Powers – they *really* hate each other.'

Atti peered around the edge of the pipe. 'The Powers? Izmae's a Power?'

Care rolled her eyes. 'Course.'

'But Tring said Laurie was a Power.'

'Yeah, course.'

'But—' His words were snatched away by the spit of melting metal. A white flash blinded him for a second. When he opened his eyes again, there was a huge silver wound in the red pipe above them.

The pipe shuddered and started to spit hot water all around them.

The crowd around them surged, pushing forward, collapsing into each other in a blur of red laser shots and flying fists.

'Out!' Care shouted. 'Quick!'

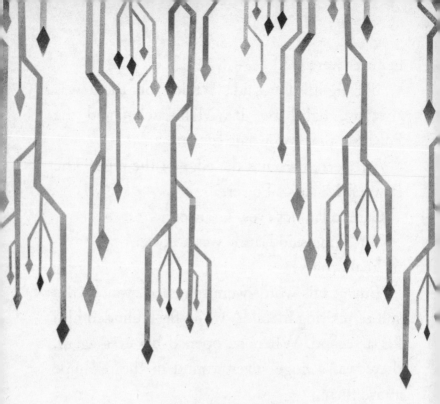

ESCAPE

Railey jumped out from under the cover of the pipe just as a lump of melted metal slid down to the deck by their feet.

Care pulled her close. 'This is a big fight,' she said, releasing a blast from her taser into the thigh of a Junker.

Railey ducked as a laser blasted into the deck a few metres away. 'OK, let's get back to the ship.'

Care shook her head. 'Nope.'

'What?'

'Look.' She pointed past them.

The pipe they'd hidden under had been punctured several times by the laser cutters, and was gushing boiling water in great plumes along the deck, blocking the way back to the stairs.

'What do we do?'

Care lifted her taser in an arc and brought it down in the face of a Junker who was running towards them. She side-stepped around his falling body and peered over the edge of the ship.

'We go this way,' she said, putting a hand on the ship's railing.

'Over the edge?' Railey ducked to avoid a MagBoot that had been launched into the air. 'Are you crazy?'

Care dug into her overall pockets and threw a pair of gloves at Railey. 'Yup. We go gecko style,' she said, with a wink at Atti.

The tiny girl spun back and shot bursts of electricity from the taser into the crowd. The brawl had spread out, and was now licking at their heels. Then she smiled and fell over the side.

Terrified, Railey shoved the magnetic gloves over her shaking hands and began to climb on to the railing.

'Oi!'

A voice rang out above all the others, distorted by the organ pipe.

Railey froze.

'Get that girl!' Izmae screamed from the turret, her whole head shoved inside the organ pipe so her screaming voice shook the Sphereship's walls. 'Get that filthy little Boxville rat!'

The Junkers on the deck hesitated, turning their scarred faces towards Railey.

Care's hand appeared from the other side of the railing – Railey felt a sharp pull, and her world turned sideways. Before her brain could calculate what had happened, she found herself staggering down the sheer side of the gigantic ship.

Railey felt sick. Everything was tilted the wrong way. The Soup glittered to her right and the deep blue/black of Earth fell away to her left. Her body wanted to be upright and her ankles protested at the angle so much Railey felt they would break.

'Use your arms more!' Care shouted. 'Move like a gecko.'

'Crawl, Railey,' Atti said in her ear. 'Right hand and left foot, then vice versa.'

Railey pushed her bum out and felt the pressure in her ankles lessen. She crawled along behind Care, who was moving so gracefully it was like she was part gecko herself.

The Junkers began to pour over the railing, stumbling and slipping and grappling down the side of the hull as they made their pursuit.

'They're going to catch us!' Atti squeaked.

'No they're not.' Care veered sharply upwards, pulling them back up the ship towards the railing, where the huge items of junk were tethered. Railey followed, breathlessly, her whole body screaming at her to stop.

'Up here!' Care shouted. 'Quicker!'

Care jumped off the hull and up on to one of the thick tethers that held the junk to the ship.

Railey attempted to jump after her, but her MagBoots refused to leave the hull.

'You have to jump!' Care shouted.

'I know that!' Railey screamed back. 'But my boots are stuck to the deck.'

'Well, switch them off!'

'How?'

Care jabbed the heel of her boot into the tether twice. The lights on the sole changed to blue. 'There.'

Railey did the same and felt the world tumble away from her.

'Not now! When you jump! Ugh, what a dumbo!' Care cried.

Atti clung to Railey's ear as they cartwheeled down the side of the ship. Railey held out her hands with her palms spread, hoping to gain a hold, but the magnets in the gloves were too weak to work at that speed.

Then she felt Care's hand on her collar again, and she was flung violently upwards, on to the roof of the double-decker bus that was hanging on the end of the tether.

Railey tapped the heels to reactivate the boots.

Care rubbed her arm. 'You're so heavy,' she sulked. 'Nearly pulled it out the socket.'

The world was the right way up now, but they

were stuck on a floating island of junk, with a thousand Junkers firing at them from the ship.

Railey could see a line of different salvaged vehicles floating on tethers alongside the deck in front of them, and the tiny outline of the *Hover-Sport* tied up at the staircase somewhere far beyond.

It seemed an impossible distance.

The Junkers laughed and jeered – they knew they had them trapped. 'We're going to jump along,' Care said, checking behind them. 'Two taps off, jump, land, two taps on, run, two taps off, jump . . . get it?'

Railey nodded. The junk on the next tether along was a small fishing trawler. Its deck seemed impossibly far away, but she guessed the conditions here in the mesosphere made it different—

A laser cutter spat orange sparks as the Junkers began to cut through the tether holding the bus to the deck.

'GO!' Care cried, launching herself forward and sailing through the air, landing on the trawler's deck with the grace of a ballerina.

Railey tapped her boots and ran two steps

before launching herself after her. As her MagBoots left its roof, the bus began to topple down the ship into the abyss below.

She landed on the deck of the trawler with a thud and rolled into Care's skinny legs.

'Get up!' the girl shouted, already springing over the railing to the other side. Panting, Railey tapped her boots and followed, dodging the bright flashes of the laser cutters as they went.

That was the rhythm then: yellow school bus – double tap, run, double tap, and jump. Dumper truck – double tap, run, double tap, jump. Grain silo – double tap, run, double tap, jump . . .

The Junkers rushed at them from all sides – climbing the tethers, running along the deck and swarming up the hull of the ship. Railey focused on the strange dance, knowing one mistake would mean falling back to Earth.

They landed on the last tethered object before the staircase – a huge airliner with 'UNITED STATES OF AMERICA' written in faded letters on the fuselage – and skidded to a stop right in front of the mohawk of Razor and the rest of Izmae's clan.

Razor was holding a circular laser cutter, spinning with vicious red sparks.

'Where you gonna go now, little sky squirrels?' the Junker smiled. 'Nowhere left to jump?'

Railey felt a soft tap on her neck. 'Below you,' Atti whispered. Railey glanced at her feet, and noticed an orange tungsten glow coming from somewhere below.

'Care . . .' she said, stepping back. The girl didn't turn, but Railey saw her body tense up, ready. 'TAP TAP JUMP BACK!' Railey shouted, before doing the same.

She tapped the heels of her MagBoots twice and fell away down the side of the plane. At the same time she flung her body forward, grabbing hold of the open aircraft door. She caught Care as she sailed past and pulled her inside, before pulling the door closed behind them.

The interior of the plane was covered in thick carpet and plush leather, and was still lit by cosy tungsten lights.

Railey and Care tumbled along the narrow passageways as the sound of stomping, confused Junkers echoed overhead.

'They don't know we're here,' Atti whispered.

'They'll figure it out soon,' Railey panted.

'Razor won't,' Care said, punching each window as she passed to see if any would open. 'But Izmae will.'

When they got to the end of the plane, they entered a room lined with screens and comfortable-looking chairs that, by the look of it, Izmae's clan must have been stripping of its wiring.

Railey kicked the door beside it and it yawned open, revealing the black of the mesosphere and the tiny speck of the *HoverSport* docked far below.

She pulled back and swallowed something slimy and sour in the back of her throat. The side of the *Knock* was still too far away – they'd never make the jump. She put her hands to her head, trying to think.

'We've got to jump,' Care said. 'But stick your boots out towards our ship.'

'We'll fall.'

'Well yeah, we're not going to fly.'

Railey swallowed her frustration back. She had worse things than Care's sarcasm to worry about now.

Care glanced back at the corridor.

'This one is tap tap, jump, tap tap. OK? You've got to switch them on in the air, then they'll help drag you to the ship.'

The footsteps above were loud and pounding now.

Railey pulled her visor down, and felt her neck. Her stomach flipped.

'Oh no.'

Care jumped around. 'What? Where?!'

'No.' Railey's fingers pawed around the back of her neck. 'My goggles. Atti, they're gone!'

Care pulled Railey back to the door. 'Pay attention.'

Railey shrugged her away. She thrust her hand inside her collar and around the helmet. Still, there was no sign of the goggles.

'They're not here,' Atti said.

'No,' Railey cried. 'No, no. Gran's goggles, Atti!'

Care grabbed Railey's hands and held them down by her sides.

'Listen, dummy—' she began, but Railey cut her off.

'No, you listen, Care. Those goggles are all we've got left of Gran—'

'Well, you should have taken better care of them then.'

Railey gasped. 'Would it hurt you to be nice to me for once?'

Care shrugged. 'Maybe I would, if you stopped being so *bad* at *everything*.'

Railey felt white-hot all over. Care was grinning and it was making her want to push her out of the doorway, MagBoots ready or not.

The sound of footsteps was inside the plane now. Muffled to soft thuds by the carpet. Close.

Atti pulled on her ear. 'Railey,' he said, knowing her more than she knew herself, 'don't say anything –'

'Oh really? We could easily do the plan without *you*,' Railey snapped at Care.

'—you'll regret,' Atti finished, with a shake of his head.

Care's pale cheeks flushed.

'All you do is make smart comments and eat sugar!' Railey shouted. 'I can engineer, and Atti can fly. What's Laurie even got you on the ship for, hey? Apart from feeling sorry for you— Ow!'

Care had pushed Railey out of the door just as Razor came into view at the end of the corridor.

'Care!' Railey screamed.

She wheeled in the air for a second, then tapped the heels of her boots together. The soles flicked to red and instantly she could feel the boots attracting to the *HoverSport* below.

With the last bits of strength she had, she kept her legs straight and let the magnets in her boots work like a rudder, guiding her towards the deck of the Sphereship.

She landed with a thud, rolled twice and came to a stop in the middle of a heap piled with nuts and bolts that clattered to the ground around her.

'It worked!' she cried, and hugged the cold, hard metal deck. 'It worked!'

Tring was instantly beside her, his screen glowing red. 'Are you all right?' he asked, picking through her clothes with his pincer.

'We're fine,' Atti said, wobbling out of Railey's pocket and falling back on the metal.

Laurie rushed over, his cheeks red with anger. 'I gave an ORDER to stay on the ship.'

'Where's Care?' Railey asked, shaking the stars out of her eyes and looking around, then up.

The colour drained from Laurie's face.

'We thought she was with you.'

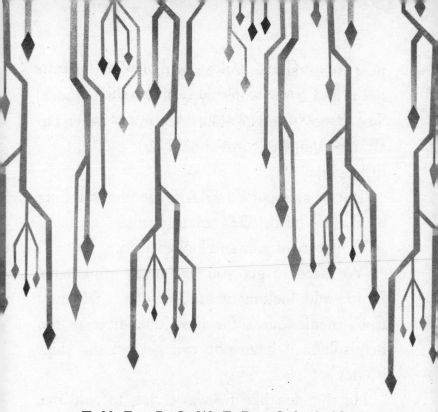

THE POWER CLAN

Railey didn't feel the vibration of the Sphere-ship's engines until she got to her feet.

'Where are we going?' she shouted, watching the code scramble across Tring's screen as he talked to the ship's engines.

'Got to get away,' he said, distractedly. 'There are severe storm clouds forming over the mountains above the Boxville desert. Izmae won't go near mountains – too close to the ground for her – and gyros won't fly well in storm clouds. The *HoverSport* won't like it too much either, I'm afraid – but the storm should hide us . . . for a little while.'

'But what about Care?' Atti shouted, standing on Railey's head. 'She's still up there.'

Tring turned grey and looked away.

'We need to get you two away from here,' Laurie said, looking at the *Knock* as it fell away from them. 'Care's the best junk diver in the hemisphere – if anyone can get off the ship, it's her.'

He sounded like he was trying to convince himself.

Railey couldn't believe he'd just leave her. Care was a lot of things, but she was still a tiny nine-year-old girl.

'But—' she began, but the buzz of a laser blast cut her off. It exploded into a heap beside them, spraying the Clearing in bouncing bicycle wheels.

Above them, the *Knock* was a mass of heaving bodies and flying sparks.

Railey's stomach sank.

Their secret was out. Every Junker in the hemisphere knew who they were now. Despite the cover of the clouds and the mountains, Railey felt like there was nowhere left to hide.

When they finally reached the cover of the storm clouds, Tring dropped the engines and they began to float through the rocky mountain range that edged the Boxville desert.

The mountains broke through the clouds in vast dark triangles, looming over the ship on all sides.

It was strange, for someone who'd grown up in cluttered, claustrophobic Boxville, that they made Railey feel trapped.

Laurie appeared back in the Clearing, the look on his face stormy. 'There's damage at the rear,' he said to Tring, 'it didn't reach the engines but it'll need patching up. Apart from that, the ship's OK.'

He walked past Railey and Atti without looking at them. Railey's stomach sank into her boots.

'Laurie—' she began, but he held a hand up.

'You went on to a ship crawling with Junkers and expected to just walk back? Did you Boxville kids really think you're so clever that you could get away with something like that?'

'Razor was here, on the ship, looking for us—' Railey began, but the look in Laurie's eyes made her stop.

'So you thought you had more of a chance on the *Knock*? Really? Care knows these heaps better than anyone, you couldn't find somewhere to hide?'

Railey shook her head.

Laurie's voice was different, his face was uglier, the rings around his eyes more pronounced.

'We didn't mean—'

Laurie shrugged. 'Save your excuses for the people down there. Save them for Care – if she ever makes it back.' His voice cracked.

'But you said . . .'

Laurie was walking away again. Railey felt anger flush through her like a flare.

'Hey!' she shouted, stomping after him. 'You're right,' she said, pulling his shoulder so he turned around. 'We didn't think. But that isn't because we were trying to be big or clever or anything like that.'

She prodded Laurie's chest with her finger.

'We didn't think because we're scared. More scared than we've ever been!'

Angry tears were welling in her eyes now, but she didn't care. 'Because two days ago we was racing in the series, and we had a Gran, and a home, and a city where we knew what was what. We didn't have Sphereships and MagBoots and Junk Bombs and stinking Izmae. We didn't have to think about anything but winning!'

Laurie was still as stone.

'In the last two days,' she continued, trying to keep her voice from breaking, 'we lost our Gran, our races and our city, and we're here flying in the middle of the clouds with a load of people we don't know, with all the Junkers in the sky after our blood.' Her voice was spiralling higher and higher. 'Two days isn't enough to get ready for this. For that!' She pointed up at the sky. 'For them! For you, even. We don't even know who you are, do we?'

Laurie just stared at her.

'Care being gone is making me sick to my stomach, honest. But you can't blame us for everything.'

'You disobeyed an order,' Laurie said, carefully. 'And now Izmae will hunt us down before we can do anything about the Junk Bomb.'

He was goading her, but Railey ignored it.

'Care said Izmae was a Power,' she said slowly, 'and you're a Power too, so that makes you and her family. When were you going to tell us that your own family made that Junk Bomb?'

Laurie was shaking.

'She's my sister,' he said quietly. 'Izmae is my sister.'

'She's your *sister*?' Atti said.

'Half-sister,' the Junker quickly corrected.

Railey sat down heavily in the dust. The anger knocked out of her. 'Spheres above.'

Laurie sat down next to her. The clouds that clung to the ship started to rain a fine mist down on them. It clung to Laurie's rusty hair in little beads.

Atti licked the water droplets off his face and

watched Laurie. The boy Junker pulled his legs to his chest and put his head on his knees.

'My dad left the *Knock* to form a new clan here,' Laurie said, talking to his legs. 'He wanted to chart the Soup – and there was no doing that from a ship as big as the *Knock* with a clan as crazy as the Powers to lead . . . and, well, his other kids didn't like that too much.'

'That's why she talks to you like that,' Railey said, thinking back to that moment in the Clearing when Izmae had first looked at Laurie. 'Atti's as close to a brother as I got and he talks to me like that. That's what was bugging me about her – only brothers and sisters do that – like it don't matter how different you are, or how much you hate each other, they still have to care about you anyway.'

Laurie smiled sadly. 'Izmae doesn't care about me. She doesn't care about anyone, especially when they're family.'

Atti cocked his head to the side. 'What happened?'

'Junkers don't fall off heaps any more. Not with MagBoots and jetpacks and tethers. Dad was careful, and he was too preoccupied with his scope to go to the heaps often anyway.'

Railey's mouth fell open. 'She didn't . . .'

'Dad fell off a heap the same day he'd refused to hand the leadership of the clan to her. Nero was the heir – he was the oldest – but he went on a salvage trip to the southern hemisphere—'

'Did he come back?'

'Some of him did.'

Railey gasped.

'Izmae's grandad – our grandad,' Laurie corrected himself, 'wanted war with Glass City. She was the only one that listened to him, that believed his stories of this Junk Bomb that he'd started. Ever since she found out about it, it was all she wanted to do; use Dad's charts to track it and the rest of our clan to plan for the territory grab after. She was obsessed.'

Laurie got up and dusted off his jeans. 'You want to know the only thing my family ever taught me that was worth anything?'

'What?'

'Don't ever get in between my sister and what she wants.'

He disappeared down the path and into the heaps. 'That drone won't build itself –' he shouted back – 'no point watching the clouds. Someone will find us eventually. Let's hope it's Care.'

Railey nodded, but she was thinking of the other thing Laurie had said:

Don't ever get in between my sister and what she wants.

She looked up at the clouds. Faded sunlight was peeking in and out as they drifted past.

Izmae wanted to rule the ground as well as the sky.

And the only ones in her way were three kids, a robotic gecko and an AI older than Boxville.

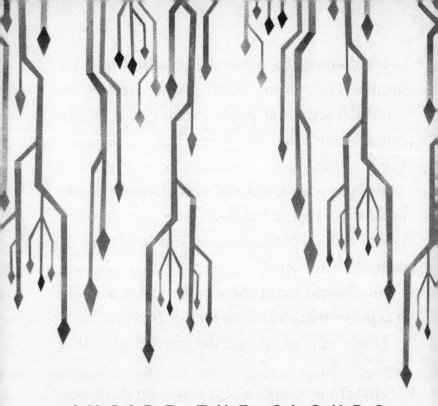

INSIDE THE CLOUDS

'This quiet will kill me before the Junk Bomb does,' Railey said, tossing a radio alarm clock into the air and watching it disappear into the clouds.

Dawn had just broken over the deck of the *HoverSport*, washing the edges of the clouds in lavender and orange.

Railey would have thought it was beautiful, if

her mind wasn't preoccupied with such dark thoughts.

'Well it's better than the sound of rotor blades and grunting Junkers,' Atti replied.

Railey looked up at the ceiling of cloud and imagined the huge hulk of the *Knock* drifting in the meso somewhere above their heads, with Izmae still spitting and red-faced on its deck. And the tiny, angry blonde girl that was still trapped up there with her . . .

'Do you think she's OK?'

'Better to concentrate on finding these parts,' Atti said curtly. 'There are more people counting on this drone than Care.'

'I hope she's OK,' Railey said quietly. 'I couldn't live with myself if—'

'Railey—'

'My big mouth, Atti.'

'Well, I did warn you.'

Railey sighed. She had a history of snapping when she was scared or nervous. And Care had been chipping away at her with her smart comments for days now, but—

'I didn't mean it.'

'I know.'

'What if that's why she didn't jump? Or why she didn't jump the right way?'

Atti twitched, and captured a fat black fly in his jaws with a crunch. 'Care's got thicker skin than that, Railey. She's a Junker. C'mon now, these parts won't find themselves.'

Railey sighed and started to pick through the heap, but the clouds meant it was impossible to see anything unless it was right under her fingers.

'I'll bet nobody in Boxville's ready.'

Atti raised a non-existent eyebrow.

Railey gestured to the clouds. 'For the monsoon.'

'Oh.'

She shook her head. 'Not had one for years and years, and I'll bet it'll start right on the night of the final race too. Typical luck. All them drones will be battered to bits by wind and rain. I bet it'll . . .' Her train of thought drifted away.

She felt a strange nagging sensation in her stomach when she thought about the races – like it was still unfinished business, despite everything that had happened in the last few days.

'We should be down there, me and you,' she

said, grabbing circuit boards out of the hi-fis, examining them and throwing them back. 'Out there in the pits, fine-tuning the Fox.' She sighed. 'Trying to distract Gran to stop her from interfering . . .'

Atti smiled. '. . . or trash talking Welt . . .'

'Aw yeah, that was my favourite. I bet he's full of it now – practically won it, hasn't he? Thanks to us.'

'It should be us,' Atti said.

'I don't think the others would agree with you, now they know we're cheats.' She sighed. 'I still think I'm going to wake up from this,' Railey said. 'It don't feel real.'

Atti snapped another fly in his jaws. 'I'm trying not to think about it too much,' he said.

Railey looked at the tiny yellow gecko and felt like someone was tightening a rope around her chest. No drone could carry her into the Soup – her role in all this was as designer and engineer. It would be Atti that would be doing the flying . . . and the dying, if it came to it.

No one had ever flown into the Soup and survived. In the old days – when there was much less junk in the Soup – people had tried. They'd wanted to travel to Mars and see the moon, set up satellites so radio signals could bounce around the Earth again – but each time the Soup had swallowed them up, or spat them back out in a ball of fire. No one had tried for years. The world had become resigned to the fact that it was trapped by its own rubbish.

Railey would never have guessed in a billion years it would be Atti who would be making the next attempt.

She'd always treated their plan like it was an arcade game, but the last few hours had made the danger horribly real.

She pulled her thumb over the crown of Atti's head.

The gecko swallowed the bug. 'I'm trying not to think about how much I miss Boxville,' he sighed. 'Or about how lovely life was when all we had to do was worry about Welt and whether or not the Fox's fan blades were too big for the figure of eight.'

Railey shrugged. 'That's all we have to do now – sort of.'

'Only Welt is the Junk Bomb and the figure of

eight is the Soup. And the prize is not dying.'

'I think you'll win,' Railey said thickly.

Railey was strong. She'd had to be, thanks to a life growing up on the dusty streets of one of the world's most lawless recycled cities. Thanks to having a gran who loved her and a friend like Atti, who was more indestructible than any fleshy human lump, but who Railey secretly loved so much that to her he was made of the most fragile substance in the universe. She would do anything to protect him. Anything.

'I'll make you the best drone Boxville has ever seen,' she said, grinding her crooked teeth. 'Better than anything these stinking Junkers have seen too. It'll fly so smooth and so fast that it'll make the Soup look like nothing but bits of rust blowing in the wind.'

Atti looked at Railey for a long time.

'I know you will.'

'Good.'

Atti cocked his head, picking up on a noise that hadn't yet reached Railey's human ears.

'What is it?'

'Rotor blades.'

Atti ran down the heap faster than Railey, whose legs were too shaky to let her run properly. He jumped from heap to heap and finally landed on the sorting bins in the Clearing.

A black shape was coming in fast – even for him it was hard to see through the clouds, but it looked broad enough and loud enough to be one of Izmae's jet ski gyros.

They'd found them.

It was too soon. They weren't ready.

'Laurie!' he called out, but the boy was already racing out of the common room.

Thick rotors were chewing up the clouds, and buffeting the heaps around the Clearing. Atti hung on to the edge of the sorting bin with his toes as detritus from the heaps twirled and bounced in the wind.

The driver was wearing a remade ice hockey helmet. For a second Atti was terrified, until he caught a flash of curly blonde hair escaping from underneath.

'Care!' he shouted, jumping up and instantly getting slammed back into the metal bin by the wind.

Railey appeared out of the heaps, red-faced and sweating from the run.

The gyro landed heavily on the ground. One of the rotors was broken, and there was a long trail of grey smoke coming from the engine at the back.

'Hello, dumbos,' Care said, ripping off the helmet and dismounting the gyro with a wobbly jump.

Laurie lunged forwards and squeezed her tight. 'Are you OK?' he said, dodging Care's flailing limbs as she tried to fight him off. 'What happened up there?'

He pulled back and cupped her face, examining it for injuries. Atti jumped on to his head to get a better look – Care had a black eye and cuts across the right side of her face and the back of her hair was matted with blood.

'I'm fine!' she said, pulling away. 'Get off me!'

Laurie released her. 'You weren't followed?'

Care shook her head. 'I shook them off in the clouds. They don't trust the air this close to the ground, and they won't come this close to the mountains in a storm.'

'You're bleeding!' Tring exclaimed, rushing back into the common room in search of the medicine box.

'I'm fine!' she said again. 'If anyone tries to touch me again I'll taser them.'

Tring appeared holding the medicine box, but when he saw Care's face he put it down.

'Why didn't you jump?' Railey asked Care.

The girl made a face. 'I wanted a fight,' she said, with a shrug of her shoulders that made her wince. 'So I stayed for one.' She grinned. 'It was a *really* good one.'

Laurie threw up his hands in defeat, but his face was all grins. Railey felt a stab of jealousy. That was how Gran would've reacted if she'd thought she was dead. But she had no one to do that for her now.

'I need to sleep now,' Care said, walking away. Her shoulders were slumped, and her boiler suit was covered in black dirt – she was dragging her right leg slightly. Care might have wanted a fight, but she'd not had it easy up there.

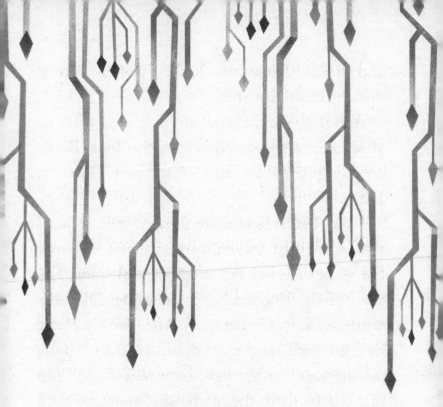

THE FOX

The next day was for healing. Healing the Sphereship with new rivets and stitched-up rubber, and healing their hope, which had been split into a thousand pieces by their disastrous trip to the Junkers' Council.

They'd spilt their secrets all over the deck of the *Knock* for everyone to see. They had gone from rumour to real right in front of Izmae's eyes and Railey knew the Junker would stop at nothing to destroy them.

And in the midst of all of this – almost like an afterthought in comparison – the Junk Bomb silently inched its way closer and closer to Earth.

Railey hadn't slept more than a couple of hours since she'd first woken up in Laurie's blankets. She was exhausted, but sleep wouldn't come. The quiet of the clouded heaps only intensified the chatter of voices in her head. After the *Knock* she had to work quicker and harder than before, piecing together the new, improved drone from the charts with the parts she and Atti had salvaged from the heaps.

The atmosphere on the ship was brittle. Tring was the only one they'd seen since Care had crash-landed back in the Clearing. The girl was nowhere to be seen. Laurie was walking around like a ghost, talking to himself about defence and weaponry and tactics and how to handle the Junkers that he was sure would descend on them any second.

Railey kept out of it. She had enough on her

hands – the changes Gran had outlined in the charts were more complex than anything she'd built before, and she was doing it in hours rather than days.

'Ouch.'

'I told you to move.'

Railey sighed and pushed her hands further into the delicate mechanisms of the half-built drone. 'Just stop getting in the way.'

'I'm twenty centimetres long, how can I ever be in the way? Ouch!'

'I said *move*.'

Atti crossed his arms. 'What *is* your problem?'

Railey placed her multitool down on the workbench. 'The weight of the engine is way too much for the Fox's rotor configuration,' she said with a sigh. 'That means I've got to adjust them to compensate, which means I've got to move the whole engine housing, which will unbalance the whole thing so you'll fly through the Soup in great big stinking circles.

'And I have to do all the calculating on the back of my hand because my goggles are gone, so everything's taking three times as long as it should and even then I don't even know if I'm getting any of it right.'

The gecko closed his mouth.

'I cut my finger, too,' Railey continued through gritted teeth, 'so that's bleeding all over the control circuits and messing up the connections and I haven't eaten nothing except a can of flat pop for three days . . . and I'd ask for help Atti, but no one on these rotten heaps knows anything about the inside of a drone apart from me, so there's no help to be had anyway, apart from you knocking everything about and getting under my fingers!'

'Sorry I asked,' Atti muttered.

Railey rubbed her eyes and threw the multi-tool in the direction of the gecko.

'Where are you going?'

'Anywhere but here.'

Atti picked the multitool up. It was as big as him.

'What am I supposed to do with this?'

Railey walked out of the room and into the densest part of the heaps, intending to get well and truly lost.

Railey had twisted and turned and ducked between the jumbled mountains of rubbish, muttering to herself about circuits and swing diameters and how annoying Atti's voice could be sometimes, when she noticed she'd walked into a part of the heaps she'd never been in before.

The piles here were stacked with really ancient stuff – boxy old TV sets, two-wheeled metal scooters, garden gnomes with horrible grins. There was even a tall, thin heap piled with thousands of pairs of smashed sunglasses.

She fell down beside a heap stacked with melted plastic garden furniture and put her head in her hands.

'Do not cry,' she demanded of herself. 'Traders don't cry. Traders don't cry.' She could feel the weight of responsibility pressing down on her like concrete. The drone was her responsibility – no one else's – and if it failed, then Atti would be gone and half the world along with him. All because of bloody fingers or a missed calculation. Because of her.

She could feel the prickle of tears in her eyes and heat flushing her cheeks and she nearly let go and gave in to it all, but then she heard a rustling somewhere up ahead.

She listened. It was coming from the path beside the garden gnomes.

A blonde fuzzball appeared from behind the heap then disappeared again, behind a pile of steering wheels. Railey flicked her fringe out of her eyes and got to her feet.

'Care?'

Nothing.

Railey walked to the spot where the girl had disappeared and found herself on a path where the heaps had been decorated on both sides with mirrors – car wing mirrors, vanity cases, polished tins – all hanging off the heaps at angles so they caught the diffused light of the sun as it battled to break through the clouds.

'Care? Is that you?'

'You're too early,' the girl sighed, then added, 'but I suppose that's OK. This way . . .'

'Early for what?'

Railey followed Care's voice down the path

and finally arrived at a big clearing in the heaps.

Mirrors and metallic components had been welded together into intricate shapes that looked like snowflakes. They decorated the heaps that edged the clearing and sparkled in the faint light of the sun, casting spots on to the walls of the rusty container plonked at its centre.

The container's flakey orange walls had been etched with delicate swirling patterns, and its doorway was framed by colourful wires that had been braided together to form a curtain.

Railey turned in circles, taking it all in.

The junk artists in Boxville were good, but they had nothing on this.

Care's face emerged from inside the container. 'You coming, then?'

Dumbfounded, Railey followed Care inside.

Colourful Plexiglas had been drilled into the ceiling, shining patches of coloured light into the room. The walls were lined with shelves bursting with half-made junk creations, jostling for space with fat-leaved succulents, potted into old plastic bottles and computer housings. Some were flowering in cheerful pinks and yellows. Their scent hung heavy in the air, mingling with Care's usual smell of sweat and rust and sugar.

The little girl was at the far end of the room, bent over with her back to Railey, rummaging around in a box.

Care was still wearing the filthy, burnt overall and there was still blood stuck in the back of her hair. But she wasn't limping any more, and she seemed to move with her usual cat-like smoothness.

'Sit down,' she said, without turning.

Railey sat on a metal chair that had been carved with strings of flowers. She was still struggling to take it all in. How could a little monster like Care create something so beautiful? With the smell and the colours and the heat of the sun, this was the closest to paradise that Railey had ever been.

'How long did all this take?' Railey asked, running her fingers along the intricate petals of the carving on the chair leg.

Care stopped rummaging and looked up.

'None of your business,' she said, picking something up from the table and holding it at arm's length so Railey couldn't see.

'You're better with a soldering iron than me,' Railey admitted.

'I'm better at *everything*.'

Railey nodded and something twisted deep in her stomach.

'Care, what I said on the ship—'

'Shush.' Care was hugging the object to her chest and swaying from side to side.

'It's just sometimes, when I'm scared, or nervous, I say things I don't mean—'

'Stop talking, pleeease.'

Railey stood up and went over to Care, who was all hair from bending over. She shot out a hand.

'Stay back.'

Railey stopped. She could hear Care mouthing words under her breath; her big eyes closed in concentration.

After a second they sprang open and the girl pirouetted towards her.

'I get word scramble,' she said, looking at the floor. 'When I think about important stuff all the words get scrambled in my head and come out the wrong way.'

'That's OK.' Railey's attention was taken by the object covered up in Care's arms.

Care took two heavy breaths and let go of the object a little.

'What's that?' Railey asked.

'It's—' The girl took a deep breath and closed her eyes again. 'It's for you, numbhead.' Care opened her arm slightly, revealing a rust-red fox's head.

Railey held out her hand, but before she could touch the fox, Care pulled it away. 'If you don't want it, throw it in the recycler.'

Railey reached out again and took it before Care lobbed it in there herself. 'No, no. I . . .'

Railey glanced up at Care and then ran her fingers over the fox's face. It was a mask. Its expression was fixed in a defiant snarl.

Care squeezed her body together. 'You said it was called the Fox,' she said. 'Your drone . . . thing. So I remade one.'

Railey stayed very still.

Care flapped her arms at her sides and fiddled with her Taser.

'I've never seen a real live fox before. Only pictures. I've probably got it all the wrong way around.'

Railey felt as if her throat had been welded together. She coughed. Words thudded through her head, but none would come out.

The mask was the most beautiful thing she'd ever seen.

The snarling face was made up of thin strands of iron, each rusted into different hues of yellow, brown and red, like autumn leaves. Its nose was rubber, the ears iridescent solar cells folded into shape, the white ruff under the jaw fine strips of polished chrome. Railey turned the mask around and gasped. Gran's goggles nestled inside a honeycomb of finely stitched foam.

'You stayed to get my goggles?'

'I can strip it back if you hate it,' Care said.

Railey shook her head. 'I don't hate it.'

'You don't like it though. I can tell.'

'How?'

'Duh. People don't cry when they like things.'

Railey wiped her cheek.

'Care . . .'

'What?'

She looked up and met Care's bruised eyes. She realized then that Care was so much more than a mouthy little girl – she was fearless and beautiful and strong and talented and a million other things too. What she'd said to her on the ship couldn't have been more wrong.

Railey stepped forward and hugged her tight.

It only took a second for Care to start wailing in protest. Railey let go and wiped her eyes with her sleeve.

'If you were trying to kill me,' Care growled, 'it didn't work.'

Railey smiled. 'Thank you.'

She pulled the mask over her head. It fit perfectly. She turned and caught her reflection. The masked face that stared back was strong and defiant and beautiful.

Railey felt like she could win the drone series, get a deal with the trickiest traders in the Junk Market, outrun Nox and Izmae and Razor and whoever else got in her way, and maybe even save the world. The mask held her gran's precious SmartGoggles, but with an added layer of Railey. She felt pride swell in her chest.

'You like it, then?'

She nodded. 'Yeah. It'll do.'

Care scuffed her boots on the floor. 'I've got pop, if you want one?'

'You've had pop in here all this time?'

Care smiled. 'I don't share, normally.'

The pop was ice cold and Railey drank the whole biocarton in three gulps.

Care smiled wickedly. 'You're making yourself into a bomb drinking it like that.'

Railey grinned. 'I'm a human Junk Bomb.'

Care screwed up her face. 'Ew, I don't want to be around when you go off.'

They were quiet for a second.

'Where did you learn how to do all this?' Railey said, turning the mask in her hands. 'You weren't born on a heap like Laurie. You don't talk like you're from Boxville neither, but you must have a family somewhere.'

Care shrugged and pointed to a note stuck to

the wall. Two words were written on the back of a dirty envelope.

TAKE CARE. X

Care burped loudly. 'When I was really little they put me in a box with that on the front. Tring got the meaning of the message all mixed up when he found me. He got his circuits in a twist and thought Care was my name. Maybe it is my name. I don't know. I don't know anything about me.'

Railey looked at the note. She'd not ever thought how Care had come to live on the Sphereship. She'd never considered that maybe there was a reason Care was so protective of her home, of Laurie and Tring and the heaps.

'I know I've got a wonky brain,' Care said, tapping her temple with her biocarton. 'Some things make sense and other things are all in bits and pieces. I can remember almost anything and I can do maths better than Tring, and I'm the best junk diver in the—'

'In the hemisphere,' Railey finished for her.

'Yup, but my words get scrambled up. It's *so* annoying.'

'What is a junk diver, anyway?'

Care grinned. 'Jumping on to junk and scrapping it in the air. You've already done it, on the *Knock*. Tap tap, jump, remember? You weren't very good though. I think you should stick to your drones.'

Railey turned the mask in her hands. 'Care, I think you're one of the cleverest people I've ever met,' she said, and she meant it. 'I could never make anything this beautiful.'

'You don't need to make things beautiful. You need to make big strong drones that can beat the Soup – that's cleverer.'

Railey shook her head. 'Not this one. This one is too hard. I need Gran.' She gripped the mask hard, wishing with every bone in her body that Gran would appear and offer her advice and help with her knotty old hands.

She stopped when she felt a cold hand on her shoulder. It was the first time she'd seen Care offer any physical contact with anyone other than Tring.

'It's OK, you know,' Care said quietly. 'You're not on your own.'

Railey didn't answer. She'd never felt more alone in all her life.

A gust of wind filled the air with metallic raindrops. Care smiled and burped really loudly. 'Laurie's all I've got,' she said, 'apart from Tring, but he's on his last legs. We'll have to throw him on a heap soon. Well, we'll all be splattered soon anyway, so . . . maybe Tring can count too.' She paused. 'And maybe if Tring can count, then you can count. And Atti too. Maybe if we're all going to get squished anyway we can all count for each other— Ugh. Word scramble.'

She squeezed her eyes tight, concentrating.

'If your Gran knew Lau's dad and hid that drawing and if they meant for you to come here then, maybe, here is where you should be. With us. Our clan.'

Railey looked out at the beautiful courtyard. The wind whipped through the metal snowflakes, sending flashes of sun into her eyes.

They reminded her of the traps inside some of the drones, that flashed to blind the pilots.

All the drones had booby traps – weapons basically, designed to distract the other flyers.

She sighed and imagined the city streets now, lined with betting kiosks and waving flags, the pits filled with every drone pilot from the twin cities.

Railey leapt to her feet. It was like lightning had struck her.

'That's it, Care!'

'What did I say?'

'That's it! We don't wait for Izmae here, we bring her down to where we have the advantage – and an army!'

'An army?' Care shouted, running after her. 'What army?'

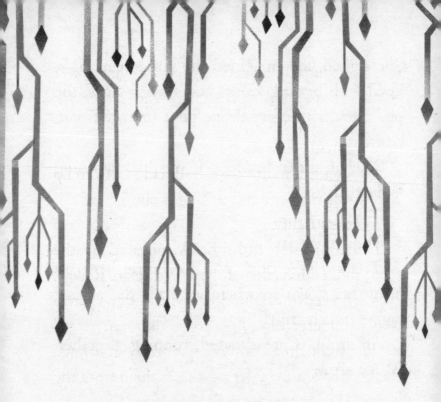

THE PLAN

'We have a plan!' Railey shouted, gasping for breath in the centre of the Clearing.

Care tumbled to a halt beside her. 'Laurie, Tring, Atti!' she hollered. 'We have a plan!'

Atti's head popped up over the workbench, Railey's multitool still sticking out of his mouth.

'Oh here she is,' he said, spitting it on to the workbench and taking his time to come out into the Clearing. 'Had enough *space*, have we? What's that?' He pointed to the fox mask propped up on Railey's hair.

'Care made it.'

Atti crossed his arms – if he'd had a bottom lip Railey was sure he'd be sticking it out.

'Where's Laurie?'

'Here.' Laurie's filthy head appeared by the scope room dome, then disappeared again. Railey's eyes followed the pound of his footsteps down until he emerged from the common room.

'The Junk Bomb will hit tomorrow morning,' she blurted loudly, as Tring joined them from the heaps. 'If your charts are right—'

'They're right,' Laurie interrupted.

Railey nodded. 'So we have to launch Atti and the drone before dawn.'

Laurie nodded. 'If Izmae doesn't get to us first.'

Railey took a breath. 'It's the final race of the series tonight.'

Tring huffed. 'Well, I've always wanted to experience the famous Boxville races, of course, but I really don't think this is the time for sightseeing.'

Railey shook her head. 'It means there'll be hundreds of drone racers in the city, all in one place, getting ready for the race.'

Laurie looked sceptical. 'Sounds great, but what does that have to do with us?'

'Izmae will attack with gyros, right? She can't bring the *Knock* down into the stratosphere.'

Laurie nodded. 'Right. It's too big.'

Railey focused on Atti. She could see comprehension dawning in his big galaxy eyes. They thought the same way, so she guessed he was thinking what she was thinking.

'Then let's lure her into Boxville,' she said.

'Boxville?' Tring turned a sickly shade of green. 'Into the city? Are you mad?'

Railey shrugged. 'Maybe, I don't know any more.' She paused to catch her breath. 'We have two gyros?'

Laurie nodded.

'How long are they going to hold off Izmae's clan? This ship has no weapons; we won't have a chance. But if we go to the city, we can hide out between the containerblocks, bring the Junkers to a place they don't know—'

Tring went pea green. 'But why bring them to Boxville if Atti still has to make it up past them into the Soup?'

'It's a distraction. If we can distract Izmae's clan for long enough, they won't even know we've got away until it's too late.'

Laurie nodded. 'OK.'

Railey was so excited she could feel her nostrils flaring. Atti had crawled up her leg and was now dancing from one shoulder to the other . . . desperate to tell all.

'We recruit the drone racers,' he blurted, unable to hold it in. 'We get them to use their drones to distract the Junkers.'

Railey smiled at him. 'Yes, exactly.'

Laurie didn't look convinced. 'Drones are a quarter of the size of a gyro.'

'Yes! And four times more manoeuvrable, and driven by the best flyers in the whole drone series, who are used to ducking and diving between obstacles! How many obstacles are there between the mesosphere and the Junk Market?'

'None.'

'And how many will there be in Boxville? The

Junkers won't know how to fly like that, plus—'

'The traps!' Atti shouted, hopping from one foot to the other.

Railey frowned at him. *Whose plan was this?*

'Yes. Every drone in the series has a booby trap – it's all part of the game,' the gecko said breathlessly. 'The Fox had a slingshot, but most have things like flashes of light and bursts of smoke or electromagnetic blockers. Nowhere near as advanced as ours, but they work, they stun or blind the pilot or knock the drone itself off course, so the other drone has an advantage.'

Laurie and Care looked blank.

'It's an army,' Railey said, getting frustrated because Atti kept interrupting. 'If we can get the drone pilots to use their traps to distract Izmae's gyros, then we have a chance to get Atti and the new drone—'

'The SphereFox,' Atti interrupted.

Railey raised her eyebrows. 'SphereFox?'

The gecko shrugged at her. 'It needs a name.'

Railey smiled. 'OK – Atti and the SphereFox can fly into the Soup without Izmae even noticing!'

Laurie chewed the inside of his cheek. 'You think it could work?'

'I'm certain of it.'

Care waved her taser. 'Um, but don't all the drone racers hate you?'

Atti looked at Railey. 'She's right. Welt helping us? After he found out we were cheating? I think there's more chance of snow in Boxville.'

'We don't need to convince Welt. Just the others.'

Atti sighed. 'The others that pretend we don't exist?'

Railey shrugged. Hemel, Katia and the other racers merely disliked Railey from a distance, annoyed at her surprising success on the race-track, but they didn't make a hobby of it the way that Welt did. They had a chance . . .

'They won't believe you,' Care said. 'They'll think you've lost your marbles, like your gran.'

Railey chewed the sleeve of her racing jacket. 'There must be a way to convince them.'

Laurie stood up suddenly and walked off towards the common room.

Atti was lost in thought. 'What about Nox?' he

said. 'Aren't we forgetting about him?'

Tring's screen faded to the colour of a bruise. 'Nox won't have forgotten about you. Runners always complete their contracts, no matter what. If you step foot back in the city, he'll be right there, waiting.'

Railey frowned. She'd almost forgotten about the Runner. Now, Nox was more of a mystery than anything. Who had sent him, if not the Junkers? Who else wanted them dead, and why? But no answers were going to change the fact that they'd have to deal with him too.

She took a breath. 'Then we'll attack him too.'

'And what if he finds us before we have our drone army?'

'Atti, are you on side with this plan or what?'

'Yes, but we have to be ready for all the variables.'

'Variables? This isn't a race strategy, this is war!' Railey felt herself getting hot. 'This is Gran's war—' She stopped. 'Where's Laurie?'

Atti looked around. He'd been too caught up in Railey's plans to notice, but both Laurie and Tring were gone.

Care sucked her teeth and sat down in a huff. 'He's still mad at you. And he probably thinks your plan is stupid.'

Railey turned on her heels and marched into the common room, where she found them both, head and screen close together, caught in a deep, hushed conversation over the workbench.

'What's this about?' she demanded, making Tring jump and bash his screen into Laurie's eye. 'You don't like the plan?' Laurie's expression didn't change.

'It's a good plan,' he said. 'But I can't leave the ship.'

'What?'

'It's a good plan,' Laurie said tightly. 'But I'm not coming to Boxville.'

'We need all the help we can get down there – those racers think me and Atti are mad already, they'll just laugh at us if we tell them the truth. How can we convince them about Izmae and the Junk Bomb and the rest of it without a Junker there to tell them?' Her voice was getting shriller with each word. Laurie was staring at the workbench.

'This is Earth we're talking about,' Railey said, breathing slower to calm herself down. 'And you're worried about your *ship*!'

'My dad's ship.'

Railey's mouth fell open.

'My gran *died* in Boxville!' she said, nostrils flaring. 'She was there one minute and then the next she was gone. And the bounty hunter that did it is still down there, waiting for us to show our faces again so he can kill us too. There's two gigantic reasons why I'm terrified of going back – but I will, I will in a second because what we're going to do is bigger than all of that.'

Laurie still didn't move.

Railey slammed her fist on to the workbench and turned away.

'Take Care with you.'

Railey stopped.

'She knows the city too. And she's better in a fight than me.'

Railey shook her head and stomped out into the hazy sunshine.

Atti was stood on the handlebars of Care's stolen jet ski gyro. The rotors were turning slowly, ready to dive up into the clouds. The half-built SphereFox was already strapped to the back, along with a pack filled with all the components Railey hadn't been able to fit yet.

Railey slammed the fox mask over her head and sat down without saying a word.

'That went well, then,' the gecko said, flicking a switch and letting a long, low growl escape from the remade engine.

'I can't even talk about it.'

'He's not coming?'

'Obviously.'

Care stomped past them and jumped on to the driving seat in front of Railey. She pulled her remade welding mask over her face and kicked the jet ski gyro into gear without saying a word.

'Here we go, then,' Atti said. 'Off to meet with certain death in Boxville.'

Care revved the engines and they took off into the clouds.

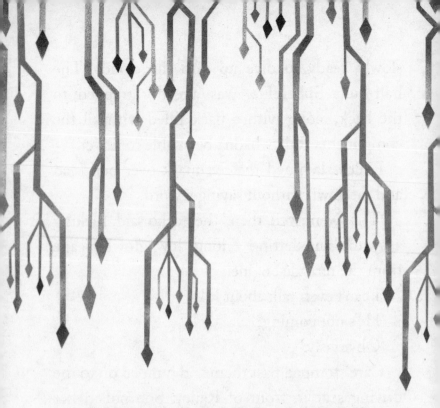

THE SERIES FINAL

Railey stepped into the smoky neon street and pulled her collar close around her ears. Despite it being only the early evening, the city was already heaving with sweaty bodies and the excited cries of the traders.

Heart thumping, she strode between the stalls and kiosks that ringed the arena with the same fake confidence she'd adopted when she was a drone racer in search of parts.

Same as then, no one paid her any attention, other than the odd elbow when she got under their feet – race fever had gripped the city, and the traders were thinking about nothing other than odds and bets and circuits and statistics.

Music drifted down from the balconies of the great containerblocks that edged the arena. Each was draped with the colours of one of the racing drones: black and violet, white and purple, shining silver – hastily dyed rags, stitched to make flags, flapping in the strengthening breeze.

The traders that milled around the streets were decked in a similar rainbow, some holding glowing screens aloft, proudly displaying the name of the drone their hard-earned money was wagered on.

There were more blue-and-red flags than any others.

'Hemel?' Atti snorted from inside her collar. 'That useless streak of oil is the favourite?'

Railey felt a spike of jealousy. If things were different, if Izmae and the Junkers hadn't stolen this race away from them, the streets would be orange and white – the colours of the Fox.

'Look, Atti. There's no green.'

The Destroyer's colours were nowhere to be seen. Welt had been the favourite before the last race, when Nox decided to tip their lives upside down. Had he been disqualified for going on to the raceway after them? Or – her stomach twisted – had Nox decided to tie up the loose end?

It would be easier for them if he wasn't around, she thought, then felt sick that she could even think something like that. She liked the scorpions that hid in her shoes more than Welt, but she didn't want him dead, did she?

'If Welt's alive he'll be sniffing around here somewhere,' Atti said, reading her mind.

Railey shivered. When had they become so easy with death? Had they changed that much in just a few days?

The gecko was right. In Welt's life – unchanged by a destiny forced upon him by strangers – the races still meant everything. He'd be here somewhere.

Railey's thoughts drifted to their own dreams

of winning the series, of buying the biggest rooms in the highest containerblocks with the prize money, of being known by every trader in every corner of the city. Now she knew those dreams were all false, carved out and manipulated by Gran and Laurie's dad. The thought left her sad and angry and desperately lonely.

She cast her eyes about the crowded street.

Everything about the city that had once been familiar and comforting was now as dangerous and alien as being on board the *Knock* surrounded by Izmae's clan.

Care was skipping in front of them, bounding around the stalls like she didn't have a worry in the world. But every time she knocked into a trader, Railey's stomach flip-flopped.

They'd left the gyro hidden high in the Tops, and had traded some rusty old pans she'd found on the heaps for some trader's clothes for Care. Wearing her new patched-up bomber jacket and holographic cap, the girl looked more like a trader's daughter – but a nine-year-old with a taser would draw attention, even in Boxville.

Still, Railey had to admit she did feel a little

safer knowing the girl had it. Especially as she had the SphereFox and its components in a pack on her back.

Railey led them away from the crowds gathered around the arena fence and ducked under the flyers' box, where a hatch was concealed by a stack of old tin boxes.

They climbed through and emerged into the pit enclosure just as the green countdown projection began to shine over the city.

The huge room was dark and deserted. The racers had already left, eager to get into position in the flyers' box and survey the raceway.

Railey moved forward slowly, taking deep steadying breaths. As soon as they'd stepped into the pits, all her confidence in her plan had evaporated. She felt sick. They were on their way to interrupt the drone racers at the worst time – right before the race. And the drone racers didn't like her much, and the thing she was about to tell them sounded crazier than anything Gran had said before. She couldn't help but feel hopeless. And if it wasn't for the gecko wrapped around her neck and the tiny, angry girl skipping ahead of her, she would have run away into the crowds.

On her shoulder, Atti felt the air shift. A blast of cold cutting through the clingy heat. A door opening?

Care's footsteps stopped.

'Care?' he said, peering into the corners of the room. But the spotlights on the workbenches made the shadows around them impossibly thick, even for his eyes.

Railey stopped. Atti felt her breathing quicken.

'Care?' she said, with the slightest waver in her voice.

The Junker was stood a little ahead of them, still as stone, staring at something at the end of the room, close to the ramp that led to the flyers' box, now glowing red from the light of the countdown.

The cries of the crowd rumbled along the walls.

The hairs prickled along Railey's arms.

Welt stepped into one of the puddles of light.

Beads of sweat glistened on his face, and his iguana-hide racing jacket, which was usually so pristine and white, was filthy and torn.

He looked at Railey and Atti with the same hatred he always had, but there was something else there now too – fear.

'That's a bad move,' he said. 'Showin' yer cheating faces here tonight.'

'We don't want trouble, Welt,' Railey said, picking her words carefully. 'We don't want to race, even. We just need to talk to the others.' She pointed past Welt to the ramp.

Welt shook his head. 'Shouldn'ta come.'

Railey stepped forward. 'Just let us past. You should come with us, listen to what we have to say—'

'He dun't care what you got ter say.'

Atti bristled. 'Who? Hemel? Oh please.'

'Who is this?' Care added, brandishing her taser. 'Shall I stick him?'

Railey pushed the taser back down by Care's side. 'No.'

There was something strange about the way Welt was standing – it was too stiff, not natural. Railey backed away a little, pushing Care back too.

Welt breathed heavily – his big hands were shaking.

The last they'd seen of him was in the workshop when he'd led Nox to them . . . Railey took a breath. *Oh no.*

'He's not talking about Hemel, Atti,' she said, blood rushing in her ears.

Welt didn't move his head, but his eyes flicked to his left. Railey followed them. One of Welt's hands was balled into a fist by his side, the other hidden behind his back . . .

Railey's breath caught.

There was someone behind him, holding his arm so he couldn't run away – someone big and silent and dressed the exact colour of the shadows.

Slowly, two round green screens appeared behind Welt.

'Well, well,' Nox purred. 'Looks like I've finally got you cornered.'

It was like someone had sucked the air out of the room. Nox moved out from behind Welt and held his PunchGun up at them with his metal arm – which had been badly patched up with tape and wires.

Railey's brain screamed at her to run, but her

MagBoots might as well have been welded to the floor. She raced through the possible exits, the places to run – but it was pointless, no one could outrun a PunchGun this close.

She braced herself for the blast that would knock them into the wall, but it never came.

Instead, Nox pushed Welt towards them and sat down on the edge of a workbench. He crossed his legs and placed his PunchGun carefully on his lap. His eye screens flicked over each of them in turn, then settled on Railey.

'Three days,' he growled. 'Three days in this sweaty *gutter* of a city waiting for you two to show your faces again—'

Railey caught Atti's eye.

'—horrible, horrible place,' the Runner continued with a sigh. 'The dust gets *everywhere*. And, can I ask, is there *anything* to eat in this city that doesn't contain sugar? Honestly, I can hardly squeeze into my armour— Where do you think you're going?' Quick as a cat, Nox's PunchGun was aimed at Welt's head.

'But,' Welt whined, 'you found 'em, now I can go—'

'I said to them,' Nox continued, keeping the gun on Welt, 'you don't send a bounty hunter to do a bodyguard's job. I'm a *killer*, not a *babysitter*. I've got a reputation to protect. I can't just turn up smiling like a floss vendor and say "Hey guys, whatever you need, I'm here!" I'm *menacing*. I *menace*—'

Care laughed into her sleeve. '*This* is the guy everyone's scared of? Oh *wowwwwww*.'

Atti leapt off Railey's shoulder on to the workbench opposite Nox. 'But you're – you're here to kill us?'

Nox clapped. 'Oh I wish!'

Railey could feel Welt shaking beside her, muttering under his breath.

Atti's jaw dropped. 'But you're a Runner . . .'

Nox smiled. 'Oh nothing gets past you, does it?'

'You *killed* Gran!'

Nox held up a gloved hand. 'No. Now, it's not my fault Boxville traders don't ever listen – if she'd just shut up and listened – but she took one look at this uniform and blam—'

Welt stood up. 'This ain't right!' he shouted

loud enough that even Care jumped. 'You gave me your word you'd let me go.'

Railey pushed him in the back. 'Do you want to get your head punched off?'

Welt shoved her away and stepped back towards Nox.

'I dun't care no more!' he wailed. 'I hate all of yer! I hate you, and yer mad gran and this cheating lizard an' everything. I jus' wanted ter race, that's all.' He put his head in his hands. 'But they disqualified me, didn't they? And now I got nothing but the steaming solar farms to look forward to—'

Quick as a lizard's tongue, Nox's metal hand shot out and gripped Welt around the neck. The boy made a horrible, wet, gurgling noise and fell still.

'Shall I rearrange them?' the Runner growled, peering at the boy's Scrabble-board teeth. 'I think I can see a ten pointer in there.'

Welt shut his mouth.

'Wait.' Railey stepped up and put her hand on Nox's arm.

Both eye screens turned and looked at her.

This close, she could see the tiny apertures inside adjusting to find their focus.

'If Izmae didn't send you to kill us, then who did send you?' she said, pushing the arm down so Nox released Welt's neck.

The Runner rolled his eye screens.

'Now that you're listening,' he said, sweeping an arm back, 'Glass City sends its regards to the Pilot.'

'Glass City?'

Railey felt the air shift behind them. Something moving in the deepest shadows.

Nox gestured with his human arm and another black-coated man stepped out of the shadows, followed by another and another.

Welt whimpered.

'What's this?' Atti said.

'A gift.'

Railey saw the legs first, then the gleam of the chrome PunchGuns at their hips. The room was filled with Runners.

'. . . PRAY THE MONSOON CLOUDS STAY AWAY FOR A FEW HOURS LONGER,' the speakers interrupted, 'BECAUSE

TONIGHT THE TITANS OF BOXVILLE DRONE RACING CLASH FOR YOUR ENTERTAINMENT – UNTIL THE CITY FLOOR IS LITTERED WITH DRONE DEVASTATION!'

'It's an army,' Railey said, light-headedness washing over her. 'Glass City have sent us an army.'

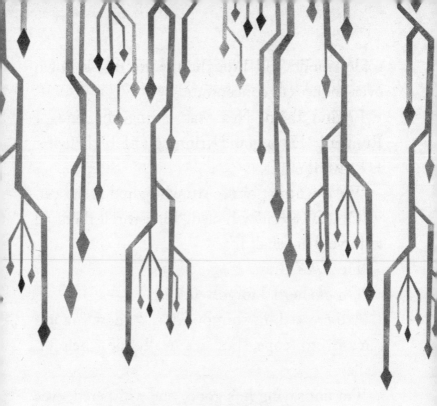

THE CASTBOX

Railey and Atti laid out the drone components on the nearest workbench. If the SphereFox was going to fly, it needed its engine finished first.

Railey scanned the parts; maybe it was being in the pits, or the pressure of the Runners behind her, but she could finally see a rough outline of how it all fitted together. She flipped the multitool to solder mode and brought the fox mask down over her eyes to concentrate.

Behind them, Nox was pacing the line of Runners, chatting and grinning and high-fiving as he went.

'We can't trust him,' Atti whispered in her ear.

'Oh, OK,' Railey hissed. 'I'll just tell them all to leave then, shall I?'

'He *killed* Gran.'

'Oh *did* he? I'd forgotten.'

Atti crossed his stumpy arms. 'I know you use sarcasm to cope, but it's really not helpful, Railey.'

'I'm not saying he's good,' she whispered, eyes still fixed on the soldering iron, 'I'm saying that, for now, we're on the same side.'

The gecko huffed.

'We have fighters now, Atti,' Railey continued distactedly. 'Proper fighters, with PunchGuns.'

Atti pointed to Welt, who was being held against another workbench by Care. 'And *one* drone, Railey. One. The fight will be in the air.'

Railey looked up at the ramp and the flyers' box somewhere beyond. She could imagine the racers inside, excitedly positioning their drones in the chutes, checking out the raceway through the window. The last thing they'd want was to be interrupted now. But they didn't have time to wait until the end of the race – it had to be now.

Railey took a deep breath.

'We're going to need all the help we can get if we're going to convince the others to fly with us. Coming from a Runner— there, finished.'

The drone was complete on the workbench in front of her, but before she could admire her own work, Atti had jumped on to it, anger flashing in his eyes.

'You want *him* to tell them?' he said, pointing to Nox.

'Him and us and Welt. It might be enough.'

'Enough to scare them away before we can explain anything!'

'Well, they should be scared, Atti. Maybe they need to be scared— What's that?'

A thunderous buzzing noise was coming from the raceway above them.

Railey looked at Nox, but the Runner was already halfway up the ramp to the flyers' box.

Atti jumped on to Railey's shoulder and they followed him up, Care dragging Welt behind them.

They crept up the ramp and into the box. The Starter was standing in the middle of the arc of chutes and pilots, her microphone hanging loose in her bejewelled hand.

Hemel, Katia and the other drone pilots were all staring out of the windows.

The crowd outside was silent.

It was as if someone had frozen time.

'Look!' Atti pointed.

The raceway below them was bathed in a bright white light. The screens that usually projected drone's-eye view footage of the race across the containerblock walls were instead showing pictures of a bright cloudless sky, pierced by pointed peaks of junk.

Railey gasped.

It was the heaps.

Somehow, the arena projectors were displaying a video link directly from the deck of the *HoverSport* – from Tring's screen.

Izmae's small hyena eyes appeared. Railey

jumped. The Junker examined the camera and stepped back, revealing the Clearing crawling with Junkers and gyros.

'Spheres above,' Atti said. 'They found them already.'

Railey frowned. How could footage from the Sphereship make it to the arena projectors? Then it hit her.

'It's the castbox, Atti!' she said, clutching the gecko excitedly. 'The signal hijacker box Laurie traded in the Junk Market when we first met him! They've replaced the arena video feed with Tring's video feed, so we can see them.'

'What?' The Starter tapped her tablet over and over. 'That's impossible. What's happening?'

'Laurie and Tring were programming something when I caught them before we left.' She grinned. 'He must have been planning this all along.'

Izmae's eyes were still scanning the screen. The other members of her clan were pacing around the heaps, kicking the lower items and causing the piles of roller skates and sunglasses and microwave ovens to tremble and crash to the floor.

On the screens, Izmae pulled back and dusted off her jeans.

'Where are they?' she growled.

Laurie was bloodied and bound, sitting in the dust with a tennis ball wedged into his mouth. Tring must have been shaking, because the footage kept blurring.

Izmae kicked dust in Laurie's face. 'What's wrong? Didn't think I'd be able to find you if you hid your big floating bin in the clouds?'

The Junker's teeth ground and her eyes were pale and wild with anger. Somewhere in the distance, there was a rumbling crash of another heap being pulled down.

Tring moved closer. 'Izmae, please—'

The Junker's hand shot out. 'The humans are talking, Tring.'

'But —' the computer stuttered — 'if we could all just calm down.'

A great crack echoed around the arena.

A dark slash appeared down the middle of the screen, which was now intermittently fizzing with static.

'Tring!' Care gasped.

Izmae put the iron bar back in her tool belt and snatched the filthy tennis ball out of Laurie's mouth. The boy coughed.

'Where's the Pilot?' she asked. 'Where's that greasy little girl and her yellow lizard?'

Railey could feel the drone racers' eyes turn to her. She concentrated on Izmae.

'If you tell me where they are, I won't have to tear your dad's precious yard apart to find 'em – Razor!'

There was another crash. Laurie winced.

'*Our* dad's ship,' he coughed. 'He was your dad too, Iz.'

Izmae shook her head. 'I lost my dad the day he became a dirt-loving traitor—'

'He wanted to stop the Junk Bomb, that's all.'

'You're going to waste your breath defending him? It's embarrassing, Laurie. You're embarrassing yourself in front of your friends.'

Izmae was getting closer and closer to the screen, so close that Railey could see the impossibly smooth curves of her modded face. She looked waxy, like a doll.

'That Junk Bomb will destroy Glass City and

kill everyone in it!' Laurie coughed.

Izmae smiled. 'I know. Good, isn't it?'

Laurie shook his head.

'It'll kill half of Boxville too.' A coughing fit stopped him speaking for a second, and when he looked back up his eyes were glassy. 'And what about the shockwave, Iz? A force like that could topple the *Knock* right out of the meso—'

Izmae slapped Laurie hard around the face. The sharp thwack echoed around the silent square.

'Don't you dare say the name of our family ship through those traitorous, dirt-loving lips,' she snarled, slow enough to make the hairs stand up on the back of Railey's neck.

Behind Izmae, Razor and the others were toppling the heaps like bowling pins – metal and plastic bounced and tumbled around the Clearing, and Laurie was sitting there, powerless, watching it all crash around him – Railey could hardly bear it.

Inside the arena, the crowd had started to murmur. A slow noise like the wind blowing through the alleys. Railey felt it vibrating through her feet.

'What's happening?' the Starter said, turning. She stared at Nox, then Care, then settled on Railey.

'What bomb? What shockwave? What's happening to Glass City?'

But Izmae's voice quickly drew her attention back to the screens.

'Our bomb will only destroy them that want to destroy us.' Razor approached her, shaking his head. Izmae snarled, then her cold hyena eyes flicked to the camera. It had the same effect on Railey as being slapped in the face.

'Then all you down there will understand the power of the clans.'

A gasp rippled through the crowd.

Izmae picked up Tring's screen and brought it right up to her mouth. Her teeth were chipped, like shards of glass. She licked her lips before she spoke.

'Think you can hide from us, Pilot?' Her breath was fogging up the lens. 'Think that stinking hot city will protect you?'

The air around Izmae began to vibrate with the thundering of fan blades – kicking up the dust and debris from the smashed heaps.

'See you soon, then. Bye bye.'

The Junker gave a little wave, then snapped the screen in half.

'Tring!' Atti cried, leaping off Railey's shoulder and on to that of the Starter, who was closest to the windows. 'Tring!'

There was silence in the flyers' box.

Railey couldn't take her eyes away from the screens – fizzing with static now the feed from Tring was gone.

They'd known about the castbox, they'd killed Tring – and now they were coming here.

She turned to the Starter, who had just noticed Nox and the Runners behind her. Her face was the picture of terror.

'What's happening?' she asked breathlessly. Beside her, Hemel, Katia and the others were staring at Atti.

'War,' Railey said. 'The Junkers are going to attack the city . . . tonight. And we need your help.'

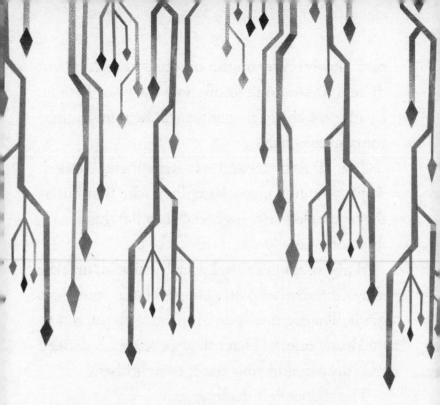

THE DRONE ARMY

'Tell them all to leave.' Railey picked the microphone up from the floor and placed it in the Starter's hand. 'Tell them to go home. They'll listen to you.'

Railey closed the Starter's cold fingers around the microphone. She stared down at them like they belonged to someone else.

'The Junkers will attack the Tops first,' Railey

said slowly. 'We might be able to hold them there, but we don't know how many will come. Loads probably. The people will be safer in their containerblocks.'

The Starter looked at Railey and smiled. 'Have you ever met a Boxville trader that did as they were told?' She sighed. 'They'll fight. This is their city.'

'They won't get the chance,' Atti said, making a few of the other racers jump. 'The Junkers have gyros. The fight will be in the air.' He turned to the drone racers. 'That's why we're here. We need your drones, and your traps, to fight them.'

The silence was deafening.

Katia's anime goggles flicked to images of pluming mushroom clouds. 'We can't fight Junkers,' she said. 'We're racers, not soldiers.'

'Why did she call you *the* Pilot? Why's she looking for you?' Hemel asked.

'Atti can fly the Soup and stop it – the bomb. In this . . .'

Railey pulled her pack around and pulled out the engine housing of the SphereFox.

'No one can fly the Soup,' Katia said.

'Atti can. He was designed to do it.'

They looked at the tiny gecko sitting on the Starter's shoulder. More than one laughed – they might have said more if there wasn't a platoon of Runners facing them.

Atti puffed out his chest. 'The Junk Bomb begins to drop out of the Soup tonight, so if we don't get to it by dawn, it'll be too late to stop it.'

'Go now, then,' Hemel said. 'The Junkers aren't here yet. Why do you need us?'

'The drone is designed to fly in the meso. It needs to be launched from a gyro. We need time to get away from the city, fly into the Spheres without Izmae and the others finding us first,' Railey said, turning the drone in her hands. 'We need a distraction.' Railey turned to Nox and his Runners. 'Now we have Nox and the Runners, they can cover us from the Tops with their PunchGuns—'

Nox smiled. 'You're welcome.'

'—but once we're out of range we'll need drones to give us a chance of making it.'

'This is mad,' Hemel said, turning away. 'You're mad.'

Nox moved to cover the exit and growled. Hemel stepped back in line.

'If the Junkers are coming I'm going home to pull the shutters down,' another pilot said.

Another shook their head. 'They'll have laser cutters. My powder gun got no chance against that.'

'What about the race?'

'Yeah, we need to race—'

'No one cares about your stupid race!' Care shouted, sending taser sparks into the line of pilots. 'Idiots!'

White-hot panic grew in Railey's chest. She looked at Atti. The colour had drained from his face. They were losing them.

'It *is* a race,' a wet voice said. Railey turned and saw Welt standing behind her. 'Any of yer can race a circuit. Rules are all the same, shapes are the same . . .' He looked at the racers. 'But get up there –' he pointed above them, towards the sky – 'no rules. No laws. No penalties. That's really flyin', that's the way ter prove yer really a racer.'

Railey could feel Hemel's eyes drilling into her. Katia's goggles were displaying cartoons of rearing unicorns. All the drone racers' arms were crossed tight, feet shuffling, glancing between Welt and the Runners blocking the exit – desperate to get away.

'It'll make yer famous, an' it won't just be Boxville watchin', or Glass City too – it'll be the whole world.' He paused. 'No one's ever gonna forget it – how the Boxville drone racers beat the Junkers in their own sky.'

Railey could feel the air in the room changing, like it was being charged with electricity.

'You'll go down in history—' she said.

'—people will know your names for generations,' Atti added.

The pilots shuffled and whispered among themselves. Welt joined them, and soon the room was filled with chatter about traps and air quality and the range of SmartGoggles in a monsoon.

The Starter was looking down at the restless crowds outside. Some had started to leave, as soon as it was obvious there would be no more racing today, but most had stayed and were still staring at the black projector screens.

'Keep the screens on,' she said. 'Let them see what's happening above their heads.' She turned to the racers. 'Let's give them something to shout for!' she said. 'Let's give them a final like they've never dreamt of.'

The Starter took a breath, then pressed the button on the microphone, and feedback screeched around the arena.

'The final race of the series has been delayed,' she said. 'Tonight, our pilots no longer race for their prize, but for their city.'

The screens flicked to life again, showing the green spinning graphics of the drone series. The crowd let out a muted cheer.

The first heavy splashes of rain began to fall on the raceway.

Atti jumped on to Railey's shoulder.

'Time to go.'

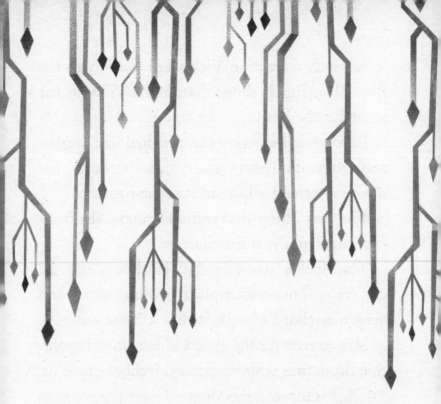

ATTACK OF THE GYROS

The Junk Market – nestled in between the vents in the highest rooftops of the city – was dark and cold and beginning to flood.

The monsoon clouds formed a grey ceiling above them, and the gusting wind was tearing the abandoned market stalls into pieces.

The drone pilots stood under an awning remade from the wing of a fighter jet, in the semi-circle formation they were used to in the flyers' box. Their drones hovered silently in the air above them.

Beyond the racers, Nox and his men were a collection of shadows, hidden between the deserted market stalls and ventilation shafts.

The only thing that moved was the sheets of rain dancing across the rooftops.

The Starter stood in the centre, looking tall and regal in her colourful patchwork clothes and bright jewellery. Her glossy black commentator's goggles were over her eyes and her tiny observation drone was whirring steadily by her ear.

'This is a race,' she shouted over the rain, 'so we treat it like one, flyers' booth or not.'

Tukker, a blond boy with a red racer's jacket that was too tight to fasten, tested his drone's traps, sending a flash of bright light over the market. Welt answered with a burst of electricity from the Destroyer's taser, and soon the air was filled with flashes and harpoon blasts and air pressure bombs.

'I want to be up there,' Atti whispered on Railey's shoulder. 'I need to be up there.'

Railey pushed him back. 'You've got enough flying to do once we get into the meso.'

The stolen jet ski gyro was only just visible on the rooftop where they'd left it before the race. It was just beyond the racers – on the other side of the exposed market.

Railey could see the newly finished cockpit of the SphereFox glistening in the rain. She and Atti could make a run for it now, but the rooftop was too exposed – they needed the gyros to come close enough that they could pretend to be one of them.

The clouds above them flashed red.

Atti looked up. 'Laser cutters.'

'Here we go,' Care said with a grin.

Tiny black dots emerged through the rain – approaching the market rooftops like a swarm of hornets.

'Racers!' the Starter shouted, bringing the microphone to her red lips. 'The race is about to begin – grit your teeth, still your heart, embrace your fears – tonight we race for the lives of our people and the people of Glass City!'

At once the drones launched up into the air

and formed a sharp triangle with Katia's drone, Dragon, throwing orange flames into the air from the front.

'The gates are open –' the Starter removed the soggy scarf from her head, and brought it down in a swift arc – 'now RACE!'

The drones launched up into the clouds, keeping formation until they gained more height – then broke off, swooping and barrel-rolling and testing traps – ready for the gyros to come into range.

'Incoming!' Atti cried.

Railey turned just as a red blast from a laser cutter smashed into the stall behind them. She grabbed Care's jacket and scrambled across the wet rooftops towards a huge fibreglass alien – the giant kind that used to sit on poles outside diners or in the queues for the rides at theme parks. She pulled them inside and peered out through a hole in the middle of the alien's three eyes.

Atti crawled on to her shoulder.

'Did anyone see us?'

'I don't know. I don't think so.'

'Too busy fighting,' Care sighed.

On the other side of the market, Nox was marching across the rooftop, commanding the platoon of Runners, who were sending powerful punches into the sky. The air around the plastic alien shuddered and rippled with the soft *thwarp* of bulging, pulsing air.

Railey took it all in breathlessly. There were more Junkers than she'd imagined – all the clans must be here, riding gyros laden with weapons. But maybe that was good – the more gyros in the sky, the easier it would be to hide in among them.

Above their heads, the drone battle had already begun.

The Destroyer was pushing forward at full speed, aiming at the nose of a golf cart gyro piloted by a Junker wearing a terrifying remade gas mask. Railey winced, but Welt pulled the drone up at the last second, sending an arc of electricity into the Junker's face.

The blast forced the Junker to veer sharply to the left, clashing blades with another gyro and sending both spiralling to the ground.

Railey punched the air. 'Yes!'

'The Destroyer lives up to its name!' the Starter cried into her microphone, unable to stop herself from commentating on the biggest race Boxville had ever seen. 'Expert flying, predicting the flight path of opponents to create chaos . . .' Her excited voice bounced around the rooftops and Railey was sure that far below them she could hear the cheer of the crowds.

'. . . And is that the Dragon above us?' the Starter cried. 'Oh! It's nose to tail!'

Railey squinted. The glossy black and violet livery of Katia's Dragon flickered in and out of the clouds, riding the slipstream of a quad bike gyro flying metres in front.

The Junker began to twist and turn in an attempt to shake the drone off, but Katia flew expertly, keeping in perfect line until she was almost on top of the gyro's rotors. With a whoosh of hot orange light, the Dragon's flame-thrower engulfed the remade quad bike.

'That's such a good trap,' Atti said. 'Shame she's never been able to fly well enough to show it off before.'

'Atti—'

'What? I'm just being honest.'

Four smaller drones had formed a squadron. They soared above the fibreglass alien and banked sharply to the right, aiming themselves at the nose of a jet ski gyro and flashing blinding lights into the Junker's eyes.

Hemel's drone, SkyHawk, emerged out of the light, spinning in steep circles around the confused gyros, powder canisters firing until the air was thick with a pink fog.

The sky around them was a muddle of light and powder and electricity and fire. Railey imagined the faces of the spectators watching the screens below – Welt had been right, this was a drone race the city would never forget.

The Junkers in the air had turned their attention away from the drones and to the line of soggy racers sheltering under the fighter jet.

'Look at the spin on that— Oh!'

The red dash of a laser cutter bit through Hemel's dust cloud and smashed into the wing, right where the Starter was standing. With a whoosh, the long tails of her coat caught fire.

'What's *that*?'

Atti pointed to a dark shape that was slowly emerging through the clouds.

It was as big as a containerblock and pitch dark, except for the four engines glowing beneath its black rubber skirts.

'The *HoverSport*!' Care exclaimed, jumping up.

Railey pulled Care back. 'Izmae's brought the Sphereship to the city?'

As the Sphereship emerged, even more gyros launched from its decks towards the Tops.

Care shook her head. 'The *HoverSport* can't come this far down. The engines won't be able to cope. It'll crash!'

Care lunged into the rain, but Railey pulled her back again.

'Lau's still on board,' Care said, struggling out of Railey's grip. 'He needs help!' Her eyes were wild.

'CARE!'

Care scrambled to her feet. 'I'm sorry,' she said. 'She's already got Tring; I can't lose Lau too. I'll bring the gyro back, I promise—'

'NO! Care!' Railey shouted. 'You can't! We need it, the SphereFox is strapped to it!'

Railey grabbed at Care once more, but the girl pushed her back inside the alien. When Railey scrambled back up, Care was already running through the rain towards the gyro. Railey could feel the burn of the *HoverSport*'s engines on her face. More black dots were emerging out of the shadows of its deck – more Junkers on gyros launching into the fight with the drones below the ship.

'What do we do now?' Atti shouted.

'I don't know,' Railey said, panting. Panicking. 'We can't wait here.'

'I know.'

Railey bit her lip and held on as a stray Punch-Gun blast rocked the alien.

The world around them was chaos – smoke and debris and cries and rain – they could make a run for it, but to where? The only other shelter they could see was being bombarded by gyros.

'I'm going to kill her!' Railey shouted. 'I'm going to use her own stinking taser and I'm going to kill her.'

A great shuddering creak erupted above them, louder than the thunder and rain and cries of the battle. Atti jumped and peered up through the clouds.

He wished he hadn't. Care had been right. Above them, the *HoverSport*'s colossal engines were beginning to fail.

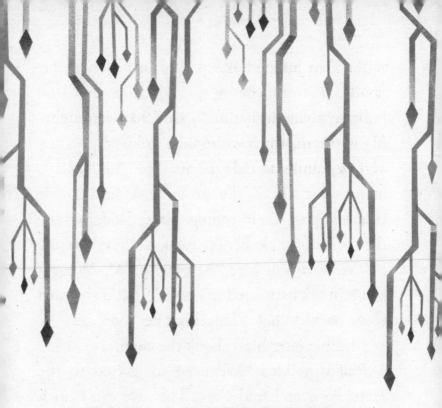

THE DESTROYER

The *HoverSport*'s rear engines flickered like a faulty neon sign. The great ship shuddered, then began to pitch downwards. The junk from the heaps – just tiny dust specks from where Railey was watching – began to slide down the deck and topple on to the rooftops below.

'Spheres above!' Atti exclaimed. 'Laurie and Care—'

'And the SphereFox.'

Debris from the heaps rained a thousand bullets on the drones and gyros that were fighting in the skies below the ship.

The clink of MagBoots brought Railey's attention back to the ground. A Junker was running past their hiding place, dodging the debris. Railey held her breath until they'd passed.

'We can't wait here,' Atti whispered. 'What if something's happened to Care? What if she can't come back? What if Izmae has her too?'

Another laser blast shook the alien.

Railey nodded. 'We need to get on to the *HoverSport* and find Care. Then we can launch the SphereFox from the ship.'

Atti crawled out of the eye hole, then a second later, popped his head back inside. 'This way,' he said, disappearing again.

'Atti?' Railey ducked out of the alien and crawled on hands and knees in the dark. 'Where are you?'

She felt a stab in her hand.

'Don't move.'

Atti was crawling ahead of her.

His gecko eyes could make out a shape slumped in the wreckage on the rooftop – it was still hard to tell from this angle, but he thought he could see rotor blades sticking out of the top.

He crept closer, then beckoned for Railey to follow.

'It's OK. I think they're dead.'

Railey stopped. 'Who?'

'The Junker in that gyro.'

A flash lit up the sky, drenching the floor around them in bright white. She gasped. Atti was sitting on the smoking remains of a quad bike gyro.

A Junker was collapsed in the cockpit, her bald, tattooed head lolling on her shoulder.

Railey crept closer. The gyro was in a bad way – the pole that held its rotors had snapped in half, hanging on by a slim thread of wire, and the whole thing was clogged with a thick layer of pink powder – but the engine looked intact.

'We can use it, Atti,' she whispered, ducking as a group of Runners stomped past. 'I just need to fix the pole.'

The gecko nodded.

Railey tried to block out the noise of the fight, just like she blocked out the jeers from Welt on a race day. Concentrating, she carefully pulled the snapped rotors up, put her multitool in her teeth and selected the laser welder extension.

Atti watched from the handlebars. 'Be careful.'

Railey wiped away the worst of the dust and traced the solder in a wobbly circle around the snapped ends of the pole. The metal oozed and bubbled and set in a silvery scar.

When she'd gone around the pole twice, she pulled the multitool away and pushed against the pole, hard – it didn't budge.

'That'll hold . . . I think.'

The Junker let out a moan.

Railey jumped back and fell to the floor.

'She doesn't sound very dead, Atti!'

The gecko appeared on her shoulder. 'Well, I'm not a doctor, am I?'

'You don't have to be a doctor to know that *breathing* is a sign of life!' Railey exclaimed, just as the Junker's hand shot out and grabbed her neck.

Railey twisted back, dragging the weak Junker

on to the ground. The Junker – still disorientated and blinded by powder – kicked and punched and howled at the air. Railey scrambled away from her flying limbs and ran around to the other side of the gyro. She threw her leg over the seat and pushed the Junker's kicking MagBoots away.

'Atti!'

She revved the engine, feeling the shudder as the rotors began to turn. Atti was a yellow dash as he ran back up into the cockpit, dumping something at Railey's feet.

'What's that?'

'Present.'

'You're so kind,' she said, pushing the Junker's nail gun into the back of her jeans.

'Don't say I don't treat you.'

'Hold on.'

Railey pulled the accelerator and the wounded gyro slowly coughed its way into the air.

She dove up sharply through the pelting rain. The clouds clung to them, wrapping around the rotors like glue.

Picturing the *HoverSport*'s position over the

city, Railey circled the gyro high and wide, hoping to bring them around the back of the Sphereship and avoid getting drawn into the battle raging in the air below it.

'Incoming!' Atti shouted suddenly.

Railey turned. A drone had appeared through the curtains of cloud and was approaching them at speed. A burst of lightning revealed the bright teal of its livery.

'It's the Destroyer!' Atti shouted. 'Pull up! Pull up! Welt'll think we're Junkers!'

Railey pulled the gyro up into a steep climb. The broken rotors stuttered and complained at the angle but Railey had no choice but to keep pushing.

Welt matched their move easily, swooping the drone under them, then circling back around so he was, once again, flying towards their nose.

'WELT!' Railey cried, waving her arms. 'It's us!'

She attempted to get out of her seat, but as soon as her hands left the handlebars the gyro veered violently to the left.

'We need to do something! The idiot's going to blast us out of the sky!'

Atti jumped out of Railey's collar and leapt on to the hood of the quad bike. He was dancing left and right, trying to signal to Welt through the Destroyer's tiny camera lens, built into its nosecone.

'Atti! Don't be stupid—'

With a lightning crack, a rotor blade sheered off the gyro's broken pole and spiralled away into the clouds. The gyro lurched and it took all Railey's strength to pull it upright.

When she looked up, Atti was gone.

'Atti?'

Railey spun around, but all she could see was thick clouds and sheeting rain, and the distant outline of the *HoverSport*'s ruined deck far below her.

'ATTI!' she screamed.

Without all its rotors, the gyro began to lose altitude quickly. Railey gripped the handlebars and scanned the sky for Atti. In her panic, she hadn't noticed the quiet teal shape of the Destroyer coming at her at a speed she could not match.

'No!' she shouted, as the drone's taser zapped

the quad bike and electricity fizzed through the controls.

The gyro went dead, and Railey's stomach launched into her mouth as she fell out of the sky.

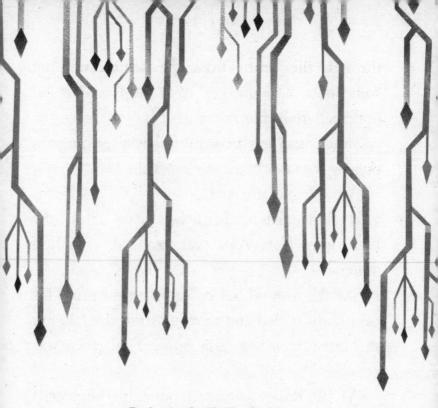

PLASKTON

Railey wasn't aware of which way was up. The wind and rain battered her from every angle, and she had to use all the strength she had to cling to the gyro's slippery handlebars.

Then, with a bone-shaking *thud*, she landed on the deck of the *HoverSport*.

The gyro skimmed along the deck like a stone. Railey flung herself out of the seat and tumbled through the debris from the heaps until her MagBoots brought her to a stop against an upturned grain silo.

She lay still in the wet wreckage, feeling pain pulsing over her body, staring at the sky.

'Atti. No, no, no. Atti.'

Had he fallen? Had he made it to the Destroyer? Had Welt even realized what he'd done?

She felt around her collar, hoping to find his cold body, curled and terrified from the fall, but she knew it was a false hope. The gecko was gone.

'ATTI!' Railey screamed, punching her bleeding fists into the deck until she had no strength left.

She fell back into the debris and let the rain soak through her jacket. What was the point now? Atti was gone. Everything was gone.

'Come out, come out, wherever you are.'

Railey opened her eyes.

'Heeeere, little dirt rat.'

She looked up. She could hear the crunch of MagBoots over the thunder of the monsoon.

'Here, ratty, ratty, ratty. We seen you fall. Got to be hiding in here somewhere.'

Three Junkers from Izmae's clan appeared between the gaps in the junk. Railey rolled into the shadow under the silo and watched them pass by.

They fanned out around the silo, laser cutters casting about like red torches – looking for something.

Looking for her.

'Come out, come out. Aunty Izmae wants to play.'

When they disappeared around the other side of the silo, Railey crawled away in the opposite direction.

The metal-strewn deck dug into her hands and knees, but she kept low for as long as she could before tapping the heels of her MagBoots and breaking out into a run.

She stumbled – the ship was tilted at such a steep angle that her MagBoots were the only things keeping her from rolling off the deck with the other piles of junk.

She didn't know where she was going. The

deck of the *HoverSport* was unrecognizable – the Clearing and the common room were all hidden in the shifting metal quicksand of the fallen heaps.

'There she is!'

Railey skidded to a halt. She must have reached the rear of the ship, because she could see the pale blue swimming-pool glow of the plaskton vats.

Through the sheets of rain, she could just make out a cluster of people beside them, backlit by the plaskton's glow.

Railey recognized Izmae and Razor immediately.

Razor was standing on the edge of the vats, holding something small out over the bubbling water.

Izmae waved like she was greeting a long-lost friend. 'Don't be shy. Got something to show you, haven't I?'

Railey glanced back. More Junkers were behind her, blocking her way back. She stumbled on the shifting ground. Nowhere to run.

'C'mon, it'll be fun – have a look.'

Izmae swept her arm back, directing Railey's attention to something small and yellow wriggling in Razor's fist.

'Atti!'

'Hey, Railey, lovely evening.' Atti's right eye was swollen shut, and one of his back legs was hanging limp, but apart from that he looked OK. Alive. That was all that mattered.

Railey didn't know whether to be terrified or elated.

'Oh, look at this reunion!' Izmae said, clapping her hands together like an enthusiastic schoolteacher. 'We love a reunion, don't we, Lau?'

Laurie and Care were on the other side of the pool, two members of Izmae's clan pressing laser cutters against their heads.

Izmae counted on her fingers. 'I got your stupid lizard – your little *pilot*. I got my traitorous brother and his scrawny little stray – and now I got *you*.' She smiled. 'I think that's the full set, isn't it?'

Railey couldn't take her eyes off Atti. He was struggling less now, giving in to exhaustion. Beneath him, the hungry plaskton bubbled and fizzed in anticipation.

She raced through potential plans, but Izmae had her in checkmate. If she made a lunge for Atti, Laurie and Care would get lasered – if she went for them, Atti would drop into the plaskton pool and be devoured.

The *HoverSport*'s deck creaked and shuddered. It was only a matter of time before the other two engines failed and the whole ship would crash into the containerblocks below it.

'We can't stay here,' Railey shouted, trying to buy some time. 'It's not safe.'

Izmae let out a howl. 'Oh no, Razor!' she exclaimed, theatrically slapping her cheeks. 'She says it's not safe! Better go home then, get the kettle on, put our feet up.'

Razor grinned.

Railey caught Laurie's eye. As she did, he glanced to the right of the plaskton pools, just for a second. He was trying to tell her something. Railey followed his gaze and saw a shape shift in the darkness.

'The rear engines are almost gone,' Atti said weakly. 'Ship will break in two—'

'You're destroying Dad's ship, like you're going to destroy every other Sphereship in the mesosphere,' Laurie shouted, bringing all the Junkers' attention to him. 'That Junk Bomb will kill everyone and everything – the twin cities and our ships. Traders and Junkers – everyone.'

He pushed the Junker that was holding him, and managed to step a little closer to his sister. The blue glow of the plaskton cast harsh shadows across his face, so all Railey could really see were his gritted teeth and his angry, shining eyes. 'You *will* be famous, Iz. But for *destroying* the Junkers' way of life. For killing us all.'

'Shut up, Lau,' Care hissed. 'She'll zap you!'

Izmae's face twisted.

Behind them, Railey watched the shadowy shape move closer.

'Any Junker that survives will curse the heap you were born on,' Laurie cried. 'Our clan's name will be as good as mud—'

Izmae made a noise like an animal and lunged at Laurie. She wrapped her thin fingers around his neck and snatched the laser cutter from the Junker holding him.

The shadow was close now, right behind Razor.

'Go on, then,' Laurie said, looking his sister right in the eyes. 'Blast me. Because of you, we'll all be dead tomorrow anyway.'

Izmae gritted her teeth, but she didn't move.

'If you're really as tough as you make out, blast me – go on, for the good of the clans—'

Izmae screamed in frustration. She turned away from Laurie and pulled her laser cutter in a great arc, bringing it down on Razor's arm.

'ARGH!' the Junker howled.

'NO!' Railey cried.

Atti sailed through the air, still clutched in the fist of Razor's falling arm.

Sensing the plastic in his synthetic body, the plaskton surged up out of the vat towards Atti.

Then, time seemed to slow down. Railey saw the shadow behind Razor move. As it came closer it morphed into the shape of a man. He leapt up over the surging plaskton, grabbed Atti in one hand and threw blasts from his Punch-Gun into the air with the other.

There was a second of confusion; the Junkers stood still, unable to see what was happening through the sheets of rain – then, Izmae screamed, 'Get him!'

Nox ran past Railey and pulled her along with him.

'Take him and go,' he said, putting Atti into her hands, and at the same time sending another flurry of punches into the Junkers behind.

In the confusion, Laurie and Care had struggled out of the Junkers' grips and were fighting their way towards them across the shifting junk.

Izmae was standing on the edge of the plaskton, screaming. Razor was clutching at what was left of his arm, whimpering like a baby.

The ship shuddered. Railey felt the world tilt downwards again, and a new surge of tumbling junk raced towards them. Nox blasted his Punch-Gun into the ground around them to stop them from being buried by the new tide of metal and plastic.

'Go,' he groaned.

Railey looked down at his Runner's armour – it was melting into his skin. The plaskton must have splashed it as he jumped and was eating it away.

Railey crouched beside him. 'I can help—'

The Runner pushed her away. 'Go,' he repeated. Then, more strained, 'The gyro . . .' He pointed across the deck. The scope room roof, with its glass dome, was an island in the sea of junk. The gyro holding the SphereFox was there, toppled over, but intact.

The ship lurched again, and Railey's MagBoots skidded.

'The engines don't have long,' Atti whispered from her collar.

'We can't leave him, Atti.'

'GET THEM!' Izmae screamed, dancing back and forth along the edge of the plaskton.

Nox grimaced, and shuffled around to face the Junkers, PunchGun raised in a shaking hand. His mask was starting to fizz and melt now – Railey had to look away. Nox reached out and grabbed her arm in his metal fist. 'She's on the rooftop,' he said, then collapsed into the junk.

Railey started. 'Who? What rooftop?'

The Runner didn't reply. The junk was starting to bury him now, but he blasted it away, then sent another spray of punches towards Izmae's clan, who were slipping and sliding on the junk as they gave chase.

'Quick.' Laurie caught Railey's jacket and pulled her away from Nox towards the common room.

They bounced and skidded and dragged each other over the shifting sea of junk towards the glistening dome of the scope room.

A great echoing creak ripped through the noise of the wind and rain. A sound like the world was being ripped apart.

Railey felt the deck slip away under her feet.

She clung on to the shifting junk. She grabbed the side of a shopping trolley that had become lodged in the debris. The ship was almost completely tipped on its side now, and the deck was a fast-running river of water and metal and plastic, tumbling over the deck to the city below like a waterfall – and they were caught in its current.

Just ahead of them the gyro was still visible, propped on the common room roof. It was so close, but the river of junk was impossible to cross.

'We need that gyro!' Atti shouted.

'I know that, Atti!'

'If we move we'll get dragged over the edge,' Laurie shouted, bracing himself against a battered motorbike.

'We can't stay here,' Care cried, and pointed to something behind them. 'Look!'

They all turned.

The extreme tilt of the ship had sent the plaskton cascading over the edges of the pool, and now a great surging wave of bubbling swimming-pool-blue water was coming towards them, fizzing and spitting as it devoured the plastic junk in its path.

'No!' Railey clutched Atti. 'No, no – Atti, he can't—'

A scream echoed on the wind.

Izmae, Razor and the others were scrambling across the deck towards them, no longer chasing but running from the surge of plaskton that was licking at the heels of their MagBoots.

'Izmae!' Laurie shouted, losing his footing and getting dragged away in the current until Care caught him.

'The plaskton can't touch her,' he stammered. 'If it touches her . . .'

Railey nodded. She'd seen Izmae up close now. She'd seen the way her skin had been modded with plastic to make it smooth – if the plaskton got close to her, she'd be in as much trouble as Atti.

But Izmae was fast in her MagBoots. The Junker jumped and hopped as gracefully as Care, using the bigger pieces of junk like stepping stones.

'That's it!' Railey exclaimed. Around them, larger pieces of junk were getting jammed like logs in a river.

'If we use the big junk as stepping stones we can jump across, just like we did on the *Knock*,' Railey panted. 'Tap tap, jump, remember?'

Care chewed her lip. 'The junk on the *Knock* wasn't moving.'

'I thought you were the best junk diver in the hemisphere.'

'Yeah, but *you're* not—'

'Iz!' Laurie cried again.

Izmae was close now, but still just a step ahead

of the plaskton. Only one wrong move, one stumble or misjudged jump, would be the end.

Railey watched the junk river – the huge cross-hatched metal arm of a crane was tumbling towards them. 'Hold on, Atti,' she whispered, then took a deep breath and cried, 'JUMP, NOW!'

Railey leapt forward and landed on the edge of the crane as it twisted and pulled in the current. She swung around, disorientated and going impossibly fast, trying to find something else to jump to . . .

'There's a truck wedged up ahead,' Atti panted in her ear. 'To your left.'

Railey braced herself to jump again, then felt a pull on her leg. She looked down.

Izmae was staring up at her, clawing at her boots as she was battered by the flow of junk.

'Here!' Railey held out a hand to pull her up. Izmae took it, but instead of pulling herself up, she tugged Railey's arm down and lunged for Atti.

'Give it to me!' she screeched, her eyes wild. 'GIVE IT TO ME!'

Atti jumped away from her just in time, and ran up into the fox mask.

Railey kicked out, cracking the Junker in the jaw with her MagBoot. Izmae screamed, but held on to Railey's foot. Railey tried to scramble away, heaving herself up the slippery metal struts of the crane, but Izmae clung on with clawing nails and scrambling feet.

The plaskton wave roared close enough now that Atti could see the plastic junk melting into its bright blue wave. Atti scurried back into Railey's collar, digging his toes deep into the thick leather.

Railey was exhausted – it was taking everything she had to stay on the slippery, rain-soaked crane. She kicked out again, and again, but Izmae's grip was like iron.

Railey whipped her body back and forth, trying to loosen her hold, then felt something hard jam against her hip.

The nail gun.

Railey hooked her arm through a crane strut and pulled the nail gun out of the back of her jeans with her free hand. Panting, she pointed it at Izmae.

'Let go,' she shouted.

Izmae just smiled. 'You haven't got the guts.'

Railey's hand shook. 'I'll do it, I swear. Let go.'

The Junker laughed.

Railey's finger hovered on the trigger; she closed her eyes. She didn't want to do it. She really didn't want to do it. But the Junker had given her no choice—

'Izmae!' Laurie was clinging to a caravan hanging halfway across the gap beside them. 'Behind you!'

Railey looked up. As she did, the wave of plaskton hit them with the force of a thousand PunchGuns.

Izmae screamed, then the sound was swallowed by the water.

Railey pressed her body against the crane, pulling her jacket as close to her body as she could.

For a second, the world was covered in foam. Soft and soundless.

Railey felt a weight release from her legs.

The plaskton wave battered her body and licked

at her skin, burning, searching, choking . . .

Then it was gone, and the wet rumbling madness of the world came rushing back like thunder.

'Atti!' Railey coughed. 'Atti!'

'Railey!' Care's hand appeared above her. Railey grabbed it and let the girl drag her through the junk until they reached the common room.

Care and Laurie hauled her up on to the roof.

'Are you OK?' Care said, her tiny hand searching Railey's jacket.

Railey nodded.

'I was talking to Atti.'

The gecko emerged out of the collar and wobbled on to the rooftop.

'I'm OK,' he said, collapsing on to the metal.

Railey glanced at her racing jacket – zips and toggles were melted to shreds and the contents of her pockets were gone, but the thick cowhide had kept the plaskton away.

Care waded through the junk on the roof and pulled the gyro out. The SphereFox was still strapped to its nose.

'Get on, Railey.'

The ground lurched beneath them.

'The ship's going down,' Laurie said.

Railey slung her leg over the gyro's seat. 'But what about you?'

Care smiled wickedly.

Laurie kicked the gyro's rotors. 'You concentrate on saving the world,' he said, then smiled back at Care. 'We're going to save Dad's ship.' He hefted his fighting wrench and smiled a smile Railey hadn't seen before.

'Good luck,' he shouted as Railey felt the gyro rising into the air.

'Don't mess this up, dumbos,' Care said, with a wave.

The rotors on the broken gyro coughed and complained as they rose up and up into the dark and rain – the battle below them, and the Soup ahead.

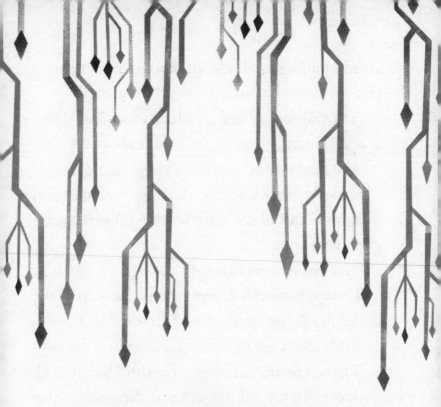

THE MESOSPHERE

The gyro broke through the ceiling of the storm and burst into another world of bright golden sun and pink floss clouds. It was dawn up here, and the sun warmed the thick cowhide of Railey's tattered racer's jacket and turned the raindrops to glitter.

The gyro's engine whined in protest at the steep climb, but Railey held the handlebars steady, pulling her body forward to urge them up faster.

Atti crawled off her shoulder and stared down at the clouds.

'We made it,' he said, his eyes glistening.

Railey glanced at the dark grey clouds and imagined the black dots of the Junkers' gyros giving chase.

'Not yet,' she whispered.

The gecko nodded, and cast his gaze up to the dark blue of the approaching mesosphere.

'Feels like a dream.'

'I never dreamt anything like this,' Railey said. 'Not even in my wildest, craziest dreams.'

Atti was screwing his tiny hands together in that way he did when he was scared. Railey reached out and ran her thumb over his head. The gecko closed his eyes and turned around to her. She pulled forward and pressed her nose against his snout.

'I can feel my atoms shaking,' he said. 'I feel like they're pulling me apart, and I'm just going to spill all over the floor and be no use to anyone.'

Railey couldn't look at him. Her heart was

tearing apart at the thought of Atti flying up into the Soup without her, but she had to stay strong. Like Gran used to say, '*Believing that you can do something is as good as actually doing it.*'

'I never been so scared in my whole life,' Railey said, fighting to keep the tears out of her eyes. She could feel Atti's tiny body shuddering. 'But it's not the first time I said that, is it?'

The gecko's eyes snapped open. He cocked his head to the side.

'You said it on the Tops, after the race?'

Railey nodded. 'And I said it in on the *Knock*, and when Care dragged us down between the containerblocks. Truth of it is, every time we've been scared, we did it, didn't we? We survived. We lived to tell the tale, just like you said we would.'

A tear escaped down Atti's yellow cheek. He shook it away.

Railey smiled. 'You're designed for this, Atti,' she said. 'Gran made you for this. And Gran never made anything that didn't work, did she?'

The gecko nodded. 'I wish she was here.'

'Me too.'

Something Nox had said on the deck of the *HoverSport* niggled at her. Something important, but she couldn't quite remember why. The gyro interrupted her thoughts with a low rumble. Railey clutched at the handlebars. It was taking all her strength to keep them in a straight line.

'We're not on our own, though.'

Atti looked at her.

'It's not just me and you any more,' she explained. 'It's me and you and Laurie and Care, too.'

She licked her lips and heaved the jet ski to the left. 'When you fly up there, you'll have all of us watching out for you.'

Atti nodded.

'And they don't really know it yet, but everyone down there in the city will be watching out for you too. You've got thousands of people with you, every step of the way – the biggest crowd you've ever flown in front of.'

The gecko grinned. 'Better give them all a good show, then,' he said.

Railey smiled back. 'There it is. Biggest ego on the raceway is back.'

Atti crawled down into the cockpit of the SphereFox and pulled the hatch closed.

He took a deep, steadying breath, and turned his galaxy gaze to the darkening sky above them.

'No more hiding, Railey,' he said. 'Now they can see what a gecko can really do.'

Soon, the broken, complaining gyro reached the top of the mesosphere and approached the dark edge of the thermosphere, where the threshold of the Soup glittered like confetti.

This was closer than the Junkers dared fly, closer than anyone had been to the Soup for centuries.

Debris began to sail past them. A truck came spinning out of nowhere and Railey had to pull the gyro up at speed to avoid a collision. When they levelled out, the engine began to cough.

'Not enough air,' she said.

Atti looked at her from the cockpit of the SphereFox. 'Time to go, then.'

Railey nodded. 'Time to go . . . Atti?'

'I'll be OK.'

Atti kicked the drone's engines up to full and

felt the tiny craft separate from the gyro. He held Railey's gaze as he moved away.

'For Gran,' he said.

'For Gran,' Railey mouthed back, before she fell away into the smoky black below.

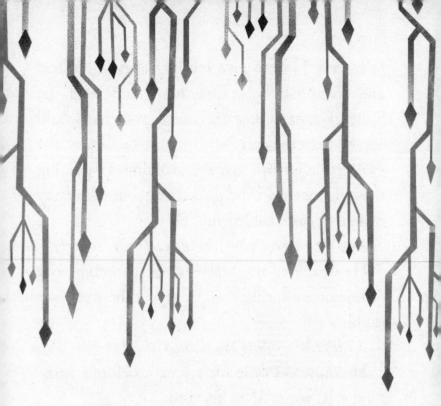

THE JUNK BOMB

Atti grabbed the SphereFox's controls and piloted the drone up into the Soup.

The relentless torrent of junk reminded him of the games he'd watched Railey play in the Boxville arcades. A little pixelated ship buzzing in between the pixelated rocks and spaceships, like a fly. But the SphereFox wouldn't regenerate when it collided, and there were no tokens to add to his machine to give him extra lives. He had one chance at this. One hit would send the SphereFox careering off course, and that would surely mean the end.

Atti pulled up sharply, avoiding a spinning washing machine, and ducked left, out of the way of a giant rusted ship's funnel.

And the Fox is flying like the east wind tonight!

He imagined the Starter's voice booming out of imaginary speakers as he zipped between the rubbish.

. . . it's like nothing could catch it!

He only had time for a breath before a spinning solar panel filled his vision.

It's drone versus solar panel! They're nose to nose, but the SphereFox is just too quick! But wait, that minibus has come out of nowhere . . .

Atti spun the drone into a barrel roll, narrowly missing a melted minibus.

Ooooooo! This is some precision flying from the pilot of the SphereFox!

Atti bit his lip so hard and so long it began to bleed. But he couldn't feel the pain, or the tightness spreading across the synthetic tendons and muscles in his arms and legs. Every circuit in his tiny brain was taken up with the Soup, with predicting the trajectory of the objects that were just smears in the distance, and with finding his way to the point on his chart where the Junk Bomb should already be falling.

There are fridge freezers and car parts all over this course! the imaginary Starter exclaimed. *Nothing is predictable! How can the pilot possibly navigate?*

Atti zigzagged and ducked and twisted and dived for what felt like hours, navigating the sea of Earth's rubbish that tumbled gracefully in space around him.

Then, everything seemed to pause.

Now for the raceway's biggest obstacle – hold on to your biocartons, ladies and gentlemen, this race is about to get . . . explosive!

The little gecko wiggled in his seat, his galaxy-blue eyes round and glossy. Lost in pure wonderment at what he saw.

True to Laurie's charts, the Junk Bomb loomed before him.

A great, grizzly, melted mash of objects. Tangled metal and half-perished plastics, compacted into the shape of an egg.

Atti was still miles away, but even in this dense band of debris, he could see it all clearly. It wasn't colossal. It was smaller than the *Knock*. Atti had imagined something huge, as big as a containerblock, bigger than Boxville, even – but space had different rules to the ground. He'd learnt that watching the Junkers dismantling junk on the *Knock*. Something as big as the Junk Bomb would fall out of the Soup fast enough to destroy something twenty times its size.

Still, his job was to sling it out of its orbit with the harpoon nestled in the nose of the Fox. He needed speed and momentum – a small nudge at the right speed and the Junk Bomb would fly back out into space, and Earth would be safe.

Atti trusted the plans of the woman who had made him more than anything. If Gran had designed the SphereFox to do this, then it would do it. He just had to find the right angles.

Atti held his breath and cranked up the SphereFox's speed. The engines moaned and the cockpit rattled, but Atti held it steady. He felt like a flea on a dog, a spark dancing from a wildfire, a bubble in a carton of pop, a tiny black spot on the vast surface of the sun.

He skimmed the Junk Bomb's uneven edges, keeping close enough to use its great mass as a shield against the other debris. His computer eyes scanned its surface, looking for the place Tring had calculated was best to target the harpoon.

He orbited the Junk Bomb once, then recognized the long black crevice where a giant ship's propeller had crashed and melted into the side of a cluster of caravans.

Atti dove down so close that he felt like he could touch the object that was about to destroy two of the world's biggest cities.

. . . He's too close! He'll never pull off this manoeuvre! What is he thinking?

Atti swooped down so close he could see the patterns of rust forming on the great propeller's blades, the faded logos on the crumpled caravans, and pushed the engines harder.

. . . Somebody describe it to me. I can't watch!

Atti closed his eyes and pushed harder and harder on the throttle. The drone shook, but Atti knew he needed the maximum speed to gain enough momentum to slingshot the Junk Bomb out of orbit. The strain was too much on the right engine and it blew out, sending Atti into a sickening spin. The gecko concentrated on the Junk Bomb – using everything his artificial eyes had until his head pounded with the effort – and released the harpoon.

The harpoon soared through the air and speared the Junk Bomb right on target. Atti revved the drone's remaining engine one last time and felt the force of gravity push his back into his seat.

Woah! An inspired spin! Poetic almost, but look at the smoke from that engine!

Atti felt an immense pressure on the Sphere-Fox for a second, then he was thrust forward, faster and smoother than anything the Fox's engines could achieve.

With great effort, he flicked the switch that detached the harpoon from the drone, and felt gravity release him a little.

He opened his eyes and saw the Junk Bomb pulling away from him, crashing through the other debris, but moving away from Earth, pushing out towards the black space beyond the Soup.

If the G-force hadn't been pinning him to his seat, Atti would have jumped and punched the air. But his jubilation was short-lived. Detaching the harpoon had sent the drone into an even more violent spin.

He's out of control! the now-annoying Starter in his head shouted.

Atti pulled at the controls, but the pressures of the spin and the Soup around him were too strong.

With a final cough, the second engine gave out, and Atti had no power left.

Spinning wildly, he crashed into the side of an electricity pylon, bouncing along its edge as he tried to get control of the SphereFox without its engines.

Atti felt like his limbs would be ripped clean off his body. Everything was a blur of black and silver and the cold orange glow of the sun blurring with the frosty line of Earth's atmosphere.

There was nothing he could do except pray the push had worked and that the Junk Bomb was soaring out into space, and that sometime soon the SphereFox would stop spinning enough for him to try and pilot it back to Earth, to Railey and Laurie and Care.

Atti stopped fighting the forces that were ripping his body apart, relaxed against the controls and let the Soup carry him along.

He was just another piece of debris in a sea of billions, crashing through the Soup and, if he was lucky, dropping into the thin air of the mesosphere before he was torn apart.

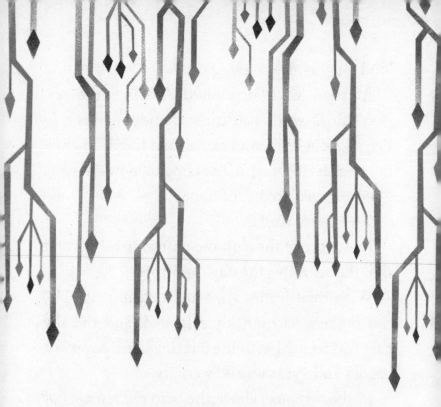

THE GREAT CASCADE

Railey steered the gyro through the thicker air of the stratosphere towards Boxville. She didn't look back. She couldn't.

Instead, she pushed the gyro down, back towards the patchwork of rooftops hidden beneath the monsoon clouds.

As she reached the troposphere, the gyro's rotors began to cut through the thick air with a loud *chugga-chugga-chugga*.

As soon as she'd released Atti into the sky, Nox's final words had come thundering back to her, allowing something small and fragile to grow in her chest. Something to cling to, now Atti was gone – a small kernel of hope.

'She's on the rooftop.'

Railey broke through the monsoon clouds and into the air above the city's rooftops.

With their leader gone and defeat inevitable, the Junkers had quickly retreated, and the sky that had teemed with the buzzing black bodies of drones and gyros was now empty.

In the distance, above the battered remains of the Junk Market, the *HoverSport* was still airborne. Three engines hummed and glowed beneath its decks – fixed already, despite it all.

Railey thought of Care and Laurie under there somewhere, arguing about nothing as they passed each other wrenches and laser welders, and smiled.

She turned away from the Sphereship and flew until she found herself in the part of Boxville where the containerblocks were tumbledown and rusted, and the spaces between them were larger.

'She's on the rooftop.'

Railey held her breath as she turned one last circle and brought the gyro down to land on top of a tall, narrow containerblock covered in so much rust it was like a layer of sand.

Thick clouds of steam billowed around her, and from somewhere not too far below, there was the smell of rotting bins.

Railey stepped off the gyro and looked around.

The rooftop was as flat and barren as she remembered it – just a cluster of chrome vents in the centre, and the broken walkway sticking out over the far side.

She shook her head. What was she thinking, coming back here? What did she expect to find? She should be going to Care and Laurie, helping them fix the *HoverSport*, or watching the sky, waiting for Atti. She turned back to the gyro.

'Who's that?'

Railey stopped.

There was a shuffle somewhere in the steam ahead. The scrape of metal on metal and the familiar *harrumph* of old bones getting up after a long time sitting.

Railey stepped towards the vents in the middle of the roof. Three silver funnels, chugging out hot air from the streets below them, were making the air on the rooftop shimmer.

There was more shuffling, and a head appeared out of one of the vents – two twinkling black pebble eyes surrounded by a cloud of wiry grey hair.

Railey felt her knees buckle.

It couldn't be.

'Gran?'

'That you, Railey?'

With another grunt, Gran pulled herself out of the vent and toppled in a heap on the rooftop.

'Oh, me back!'

'Gran!'

Railey ran towards the old woman and threw her arms around her. 'You're alive!' She buried her head into Gran's hair. 'All this time we thought he done you in, but—'

'He's wi' us, Railey,' Gran said, cupping her cheeks and looking at her earnestly. 'Nox, the

Runner. I got it all wrong – he's on our side!'

'I know, Gran.'

Railey pulled Gran's head to her chest and held her tight. She breathed in the familiar smell of floss and rust and solder smoke – still trying to prove to herself that this was real, this was happening.

'He explained it all once you'd gone,' Gran said, pulling at Railey's racer's jacket. 'Then he followed yer, an' left me stuck up here. I'd already toppled the stairs, so he couldn't follow yer quickly.'

Railey smiled and held Gran's soft, wrinkled hands in hers. 'It's OK,' she said softly. 'Everything's going to be OK.'

Gran frowned at her. Trying to remember.

'Where you been?' she said, vacantly, looking around at the rooftop. 'Why we all the way up here?'

'It worked, Gran,' Railey said, tears welling in her eyes. 'You did it. The plan worked.'

Gran was frowning hard now, eyes darting side to side.

'Where's Atti?' she said, checking Railey's

collar. 'Where's my little boy?'

Railey looked up at the brightening sky. Between the clouds of vent steam the sky was beginning to flash.

'Look, Gran, the Cascade.'

Gran lifted her head and surveyed the heavens. Railey watched the flashes of coloured light illuminate her wrinkled face. It was a face she'd thought she'd never see again. But it felt a cruel thing for the universe to give her back one person she loved and at the same time take another away. Like the two could no longer exist in the same space.

Railey remembered the last time she'd watched the Cascade – curled in the alcove with Atti, grieving for Gran, unaware of what adventure fate had laid out for them.

'It's a big 'un,' Gran muttered, staring at the flashes. 'Somethin's gone off up there in the Soup ter make this much fall at once.'

Railey nodded and bit her lip to stop herself from crying.

Gran turned. 'Better off underground. Railey?'

'Let's just watch a little longer.'

Railey pulled the fox mask over her eyes and let the goggles scan the sky. They told her the chemical composition and trajectory of each flash and fireball – but they didn't pick up anything that looked like the SphereFox.

Still, Railey watched, clutching Gran as close as the old lady would allow. Clinging to everything she had left.

The chaos of the last few hours faded into the periphery – Izmae, the Junkers, Nox, Welt and the drone racers, the half-destroyed *HoverSport* – it didn't matter any more.

She pulled her hand up to her shoulder and gripped the place where Atti usually sat. It felt cold.

Tears started to run down her cheeks.

'Hey there,' Gran said, gripping her hand, thinking she was scared of the Cascade. 'No need ter worry, my love. None of it's gonna smash over here. It's all over the other side of the city. Look – all we got ter worry about is this funny little whirly twirly thing here. Look, Railey –' Gran chuckled – 'it thinks it's a firefly, look at it loop-the-looping!'

Loop-the-looping?

Railey looked up.

She released Gran and scrambled to the edge of the rooftop.

The tiniest speck of silvery white danced in the sky above them, twisting and turning and swooping and loop-the-looping in a way no random piece of junk would.

The goggles bleeped – identifying the speck as a drone.

'Atti!' Railey grabbed Gran and danced her across the rooftop, kicking up clouds of rust.

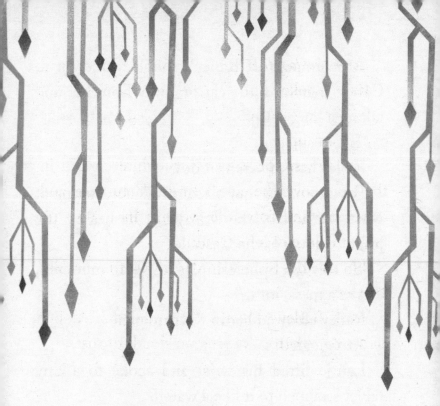

LATER . . .

Railey landed the gyro on the common room roof and helped Gran down. The deck of the great Sphereship was still, and the junk from the toppled heaps had turned from a raging river into low undulating dunes.

Care and Laurie were sat on the scope room dome, passing a carton of pop silently between them.

Atti jumped off Railey's shoulder and on to Care's, snatching the carton away from her and taking a long slurp.

'Ew, gecko spit.'

Railey helped Gran sit down.

For a moment they all sat in silence, staring at what was left of the ship lit in flashes by the bright colours of the Cascade.

'So this is a Sphereship, is it?' Gran muttered. 'Bit of a mess, int it?'

Railey elbowed her in the cardigan.

Atti giggled.

Laurie lifted his wrist and spoke to a tiny tablet strapped to it like a watch.

'Time to go, Tring.'

The small screen flicked to the bright yellow of the sun. 'Yes, I think so.' Tring's familiar, electronic voice sounded tinny through the tablet's tiny speakers.

The ship began to shudder.

Railey smiled. Of course Tring would have saved his code on to the ship's hard drive – Izmae had destroyed his body, but not his brain.

'What do you think will happen now?' Railey

said, staring up at the sky.

Laurie sighed. 'Without Izmae, the clans will probably just go back to warring about territory.' He took a sip of pop. 'The Power clan is gone—'

Railey smiled. 'Well, not really.'

Laurie raised his eyebrows.

'This ship is going to take *forever* to clean up,' Care said, jumping up and dusting off her boiler suit. 'And it's mainly *your* fault, Railey, so . . .'

As she said the words, the ship broke through the clouds and bright sunlight flooded the deck.

Gran let out a gasp.

Railey held her hand tightly.

'There you are, Gran,' she whispered, thinking back to the words Gran had muttered in the workshop. 'We're Junkers now. Nothing but sky above and adventures ahead.'

THE END

ACKNOWLEDGEMENTS

Life has thrown a lot at me during the writing of this book – a baby, a chronic illness, and now, to top it off, a global pandemic.

So these thank yous are all the more important.

First, as always, thank you to the *egg*cellent (ha! blughh) team at Chicken House for all your support and guidance, and in particular to Kesia for helping me discover my dark side and craft this book into something that I'm so proud of.

To Sandra, my agent, for being my first fan, and for your constant enthusiasm for my (sometimes ridiculous!) ideas.

To my family, and my family in-law – for being the best support network a girl could ask for. Without your emergency babysitting services this book would still be scribbles on a Post-it note.

To Liv, for being the bouncy, spaghetti-haired, string-limbed inspiration behind all Care's best bits. And to McQuin, for inspiring anime-loving Katia.

Finally to Stevie, thank you isn't enough (I know a jet ski would be enough but you know I'm still working on that). Thank you for everything.

MOONDUST

A miracle energy source, lumite, has been discovered on the Moon. The dark days of future Earth – torn apart by war and energy crisis – finally appear to be over.

Aggie, the violet-eyed poster girl for the mining company, Lunar Inc., is persuaded to campaign for a hopeful new future. But a chance meeting with one of the prisoner-miners, the darkly attractive Danny, changes her mind about everything she knows about her world . . .

Paperback, ISBN 978-1-910655-42-9, £6.99 • ebook, ISBN 978-1-911077-33-6, £6.99

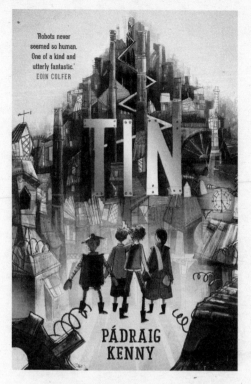

'Robots never seemed so human. One of a kind and utterly fantastic.'
EOIN COLFER

TIN by PÁDRAIG KENNY

Orphan Christopher works for Mr Absalom, an engineer of mechanical children. He's happy being the only 'real' boy among his scrap-metal buddies made from bits and bobs – until an accident reveals an awful truth. What follows is a remarkable adventure as the friends set out to discover who and what they are, and even what it means to be human.

'Robots never seemed so human. One of a kind and utterly fantastic.'
EOIN COLFER

Paperback, ISBN 978-1-911077-65-7, £6.99 • ebook, 978-1-911490-09-8, £6.99